W9-BSU-112

# THE POLAR BEAR
# AND THE DRAGON

# THE POLAR BEAR AND THE DRAGON

## Dawn of an Alliance

## DEBBIE WATSON

MISSION POINT PRESS

Copyright © 2021 by Debbie Watson

All world rights reserved

This is a work of fiction. Names, places, and incidents are the products of the author's imagination or are used fictitiously. Any resemblance to actual events or locales or persons, living or dead, is entirely coincidental. No part of this book may be reproduced, stored in a retrieval system, or transmitted in any form or by any means electronic, mechanical, photocopying, recording or otherwise, without the prior consent of the publisher.

Readers are encouraged to go to www.MissionPointPress.com to contact the author or to find information on how to buy this book in bulk at a discounted rate.

**MISSION POINT PRESS**

Published by Mission Point Press
2554 Chandler Rd.
Traverse City, MI 49696
(231) 421-9513

www.MissionPointPress.com

Cover and interior illustrations by Mark Pate

LOC no.: 2021902771

Hardcover: ISBN: 978-1-954786-04-2
Softcover: ISBN: 978-1-954786-05-9

Printed in the United States of America

*To my parents for introducing me to books, and encouraging my lifelong passion for reading. To my students who made me smile every day and taught me so much. Together, we discovered how powerful great books can be!*

# PREFACE: THIRTEEN YEARS EARLIER

The worst thunderstorm in recorded history arrived in early summer. Striking the city of Chicago unexpectedly, it grew in intensity as it raced through the heart of the big city. The super-storm appeared to be driven by some malevolent force bent on utter destruction.

The first raindrops began in late afternoon. Although seemingly innocent, they foreshadowed a sudden change. Ominous black clouds soon raced across the once cloudless blue sky. Day turned dark as night, triggering streetlights to cast their eerie glow on the frantic residents running for cover. The storm's ferocious winds pulled kites out of the hands of children. Tossed about by the winds, they spun in erratic circles as they moved upward to quickly disappear into the low bank of threatening clouds. Parents hastily grabbed picnic baskets, toys, and kids as they rushed to their cars. Ball games ended abruptly, and players sought shelter.

Lasting far longer than most summer storms, it became even more powerful as night settled over the city. Gale force winds raced between skyscrapers and through deserted parks, snapping power lines and tossing loose objects high into the air. Frightened residents huddled in suddenly darkened homes as fingers of lightning reached threateningly across the sky. Booming thunder rattled windows and unseen objects flew against doors, as if seeking entrance. Torrential downpours lasted for hours, creating rivers and streams that flowed wildly down every street and alley.

. . .

Whitney's mom and dad huddled close to each other on the couch with candles and matches near, afraid they might lose power. The storm raged for many hours outside their townhome, causing Susan to feel unusually anxious about her husband's job. Placing a hand on her stomach, she felt movement. "Oooh! Whitney just kicked! She must be reacting to the storm, too."

They smiled at one another with all thoughts of the storm momentarily gone. "I'm glad we picked that name for our little girl."

"Stan, I love how fiercely you protect others, but you risk your life each time you race into those fires. I have a strange feeling tonight, and I'm terrified something is going to happen to you!"

Feeling a bit unsettled himself, Stan squeezed his wife's shoulders sympathetically. Then, he pulled a stone out of his pants pocket and grinned reassuringly. "I've got my lucky moonstone to protect me. There's no need to worry."

Just as Susan feared, Stan got a call later that evening that lightning had struck a downtown apartment building, causing a blazing fire. Whitney's father was forced to make an extremely difficult decision, one that changed his family's life forever.

Before rushing out the front door, Stan called out, "If our daughter decides to arrive tonight, remember that our neighbor will drive you to the hospital. I promise to join you both as soon as the fire is out." Kissing his wife, he headed out into the violent storm. A sudden gust of wind slammed the door shut behind him, causing Susan to shiver with sudden dread.

That was indeed the night Whitney chose to enter the world. Susan lay in her hospital bed, exhausted from their long night. However, the storm was finally over, and their daughter was sleeping peacefully in her arms. Gazing lovingly at the little miracle in her arms, Susan sighed and hoped her family of three would have a future as perfect as this moment. She couldn't wait for her husband to walk through her hospital door and see his daughter for the first time.

However, that wasn't meant to be. Just past noon, it wasn't Whitney's father who came through her door, but the fire chief. Filled with dread, Susan held her daughter close as she watched Stan's chief walk toward her. His shoulders were bent as if he was carrying a great weight. Pulling up a chair next to her bed, he cleared his throat, looked with awe at the couple's newborn resting contentedly at Susan's side, and forced a smile. "Congratulations, Susan! Your daughter is beautiful."

Rubbing his rough hands over his weathered face still covered with soot, his voice cracked. "It was a long night, but I got here as quickly as I could."

Susan's voice quivered. "Where's Stan?"

Taking Susan's hand in his two big rough ones, he sighed. "I'm afraid I have some very bad news. As soon as Stan heard that there was a family trapped on the third floor, there was no stopping him. He jumped down from the fire truck, putting on his coat, gloves, and helmet as he ran into the high-rise before the rest of us. We tried to stop him, but he wouldn't listen. As the crew entered the building, Stan was already on the second-floor landing when a huge support beam gave way just below him. It brought down the entire stairway, with Stan on it. Several of us were able to make our way over to where he fell." Susan's eyes filled with tears as the chief stopped to clear his throat. "I am so very sorry, Susan. Your husband didn't survive the fall."

He continued talking, but Susan was so lost in complete and mind-numbing grief that she didn't hear anymore. She pulled Whitney closer for comfort. Peering down through her tears, Susan noticed that her daughter was looking up at her tear-streaked face, seeming to understand something was very wrong. Whitney held up her little hand, as if reaching for her mother's face. Susan would never forget that moment. It gave her a sense of calm in a moment of chaos.

As the chief prepared to leave, he bowed his head and told Susan once again how very sorry he was to deliver such tragic news, especially now. "Stan was a true hero and would have been proud to know that the family members he attempted to rescue all survived," he whispered, choking back tears.

He headed toward the door, then paused as if forgetting something. Turning around, he pulled something out of his pocket and walked quickly back to Susan and Whitney. Gently placing Stan's moonstone into Susan's hand, he explained, "Everyone knew how your husband always had his lucky moonstone on him. But, for some reason, I found it on the seat of the fire truck today. It must have fallen out of his pocket when he raced into the building."

After the fire chief left, anger welled up inside Whitney's mother, an anger like none she had ever known. 'Some protector you turned out to be!' she cried, looking down at the stone in her palm. She raised her arm to throw the moonstone into the trash but remembered how important it had been to her husband. Susan lowered her arm slowly, knowing there was no way she could ever throw it away. Sobbing helplessly, Susan placed the stone on the hospital tray and pulled her newborn baby closer to her chest.

Once she left the hospital with her daughter, Susan realized how painful it would be to remain in Chicago. All of the familiar spots held memories of Stan, memories that only served to remind her of his passing. Three months after his death, Susan packed her belongings and moved to the Upper Peninsula of Michigan, far from the busy streets of Chicago and all of the memories. Driving away, Whitney's mom looked at her happy little girl and hoped she was making the right decision.

# Chapter One

Strange and mysterious creatures travel on the winds tonight. A familiar beach feels oddly different. The sky is a darker black, the water a deeper blue, and the shimmering sand suggests magic is in the air. Everything pauses, awaiting the arrival of something extraordinary.

Streaking across the sky like a shooting star, a mysterious object races toward Earth with unchecked speed as if driven by some unnatural force. Approaching its destination, the object flies toward a deserted beach on Lake Superior and crashes, the violent impact of the cosmic traveler tossing sand high into the air.

A magnificent beast appears out of the sand and rises onto her hind legs to sniff the air. Towering thirteen feet high, the giant polar bear is an imposing sight. Momentarily dazed, the bear tosses her massive head from side to side and blinks rapidly, trying to adjust to her surroundings. Her huge brown eyes peer intently in every direction and reflect deep concern as she looks for a house where the young girl named Whitney lives. Locating it high on a sandy bluff, the bear frowns at her miscalculation. Her destination is much farther away than she'd planned and will cost her valuable time. On a critical mission, the bear knows she must plan better moving forward.

Dropping silently onto all four legs, the bear uses her powerful muscles to shake vigorously. The irritating sand clinging to her thick coat, and some kind of strange colorful particle that doesn't look at all like sand, are sent flying in every direction. Her white coat is now gloriously visible and transforms into dancing rays of color that shine brightly in the moonlight.

No longer imprisoned within the bear's thick fur, the colorful gems sparkle brilliantly as they spiral high into the air and spin around and around, as if happy to be set free. However, hearing a sudden authoritative command, they obey and race back to the bear, whirling around her in tighter and tighter circles.

In an explosion of colorful light, a tiny dragon shimmers to life, covered in iridescent scales that glimmer in brilliant shades of green, purple and blue. The little dragon gazes up at the enormous bear in complete adoration, with a goofy grin on its face. Smiling at her tiny passenger, Traveller leans down to whisper something and the baby nods in understanding. What a curious pair they are. One is massive and melancholy while the other is little more than peanut size and playful.

. . .

Staring at the deep hole in the sand from their crash landing, Traveller shook her head in amazement. It had been a long time since she'd called on the winds for a journey. The giant bear had forgotten how exhilarating it was to wurf and had truly enjoyed every breathtaking moment. However, when she had to stop once again to shake the sticky sand from her dense coat, the bear admitted her landing skills had become a bit rusty from lack of use. She definitely hadn't planned on stirring up so much sand, nor had she planned on walking this far to her destination.

Plodding slowly through the soft beach sand, the bear mumbled to herself in irritation, "If only I hadn't closed the portal between Earth and Yagdi. It would have made our journey so much easier, especially with such an energetic little dragon in tow!" Traveller had used an impenetrable locking spell on the portal at Ellie's Point to prevent her enemies, or anyone else for that matter, from entering. What a big mistake that had been!

Pausing to look back, the bear noticed her little dragon had fallen far behind. Sighing with impatience, she sat on a large piece of driftwood to wait and soon discovered why Aiden was taking so long. Her massive paw prints had unintentionally provided not only a clear path in the sand, but also an opportunity to play. The small dragon's huge yellow eyes sparkled with laughter and excitement as he leaped from one paw print to the next. Acknowledging her little travel companion was simply having some much-needed fun after his first wurfing experience, her impatience disappeared. When he drew closer, she smiled and waved a massive paw, then rose and continued in the direction of the girl's house.

Anxious to reach their destination, the bear turned around to urge Aiden to keep up but didn't see him anywhere. Concerned, she started to head back when all of a sudden, her little friend emerged from one of her giant paw prints grinning from ear to ear. Without skipping a beat, he ran to the next large print and dove in head-first, screeching a high-pitched version of the mighty dragons' authoritative call. Traveller knew her little dragon's youthful sound would deepen as he grew older and become powerfully compelling. Out of all the magnificent dragons on Yagdi, he was very special indeed. He alone had the qualities necessary to follow in his mighty father's footsteps.

Traveller realized she already missed those powerful dragon protectors and felt deeply concerned for their future. The mighty bear had many difficult challenges ahead of her before she could return home. Evil forces on Yagdi were growing more powerful, and something needed to be done quickly. In fact, if the circumstances in her world hadn't become so dire, she never would have taken this long difficult journey to Michigan's Upper Peninsula with such a young dragon.

Traveller was a powerful adversary, so when her enemies had discovered that Whitney was special to her, their evil hearts had developed a ghoulish plot. For the past month, they'd been terrorizing the poor girl. Every night they'd visited her dreams and tormented her with disturbing nightmares. No ordinary human had the capability to visit Yagdi through a dream, but Whitney was far from ordinary.

Traveller's elders had recognized Whitney's unique talents from the moment she was born. Based on her gifts, the wise elders had chosen the girl's destiny to be a Protector Warrior, thus the title 'Chosen One.' Now, thirteen years later, Yagdi's future king was in danger, and they hoped the girl would use her unique skills to defend their little dragon prince. Neither Whitney nor Aiden were aware their lives would soon become intertwined.

Her elders had never been wrong, so Traveller was confident the young girl's very special talents did indeed exist. The survival of her world depended on Whitney's ability to keep Aiden safe, so the huge bear had wurfed back to Earth with the young dragon and a carefully devised plan. She realized the tasks that lay ahead of her were daunting. With such a challenging path forward, she had to move with extreme caution, but if anyone could pull this off, the bear was confident she could.

Traveller's plan had no room for error. Most important, the bear must ensure the safety of both her little dragon and the young chosen one. Of equal importance, she must convince

Whitney to accept her destiny as Aiden's protector. Introductions would take some delicate maneuvering on her part, but the bear had come up with a strategy she felt would work well with the young girl. She looked forward to guiding Whitney through the exciting process of uncovering her buried gifts. She would then teach her how to use them effectively.

That wasn't all they would be asking from the young chosen one however, and the second task was equally important. Traveller had to convince Whitney to help the young dragon discover his inherited and magnificent capabilities. Preparing little Aiden for his vast responsibilities as their future king was crucial to the smooth transfer of power from father to son. Unfortunately, Whitney would only have two short months to accomplish this extremely important task. Yagdi's future king would need to return home as soon as he was fully grown, and that would be all too soon.

Traveller knew she didn't have much time and needed to work fast. Aiden's birth had been a time of celebration for her friends and allies because their future king had arrived. However, their enemies had been horrified with the prospect of a new dragon king. In recent years, they'd become obsessed with the desire to rule Yagdi. Knowing that Aiden's birth had significantly reduced the amount of time they had left, they'd stepped up the frequency and intensity of their attacks. No longer satisfied with small skirmishes, they'd begun engaging Traveller and her allies in real battles with terrible consequences. Their enemies were also working frantically on plans for a major battle, knowing it would be easier to win before Aiden became their new King. Therefore, the bear knew with dreadful certainty her enemies would do everything in their power to keep the little dragon from becoming king! That put both Aiden and Whitney in grave danger.

The lengthy walk along the beach had given the bear much-needed time to finalize her plans. Nearing her destination, she saw Whitney and her mother on the beach. Wrapped in warm blankets, they were quietly watching the sparks from their bon-fire fly high into the night sky. The bear motioned for the little dragon to come close, and leaned down to whisper, "We must be very quiet and still, so we're not seen." Aiden sleepily nodded his agreement.

A weary Traveller settled into the soft sand and patted the spot next to her. The little dragon snuggled up beside her, curled into a tiny ball, and sighed with exhaustion. A few minutes later, Traveller heard quiet snores coming from the dragon's long nose. With the little dragon asleep, the bear could devote all of her attention to Whitney and her mother.

Their conversation shocked and horrified Traveller. The huge bear was instantly overwhelmed with the unexpected and unwelcome return of grief and guilt from many years ago. Whitney's mother handed her daughter a small, gift-wrapped box and an envelope addressed To My Daughter, and the bear knew with absolute certainty who'd written the letter inside that envelope.

Extremely curious about her mom's unexpected gifts, Whitney took the envelope and little box. Her eyes widened and filled with tears when she realized it was a letter from her father. Did her mom somehow know that she'd been thinking about her dad a lot lately? She knew it was crazy to be missing a father she'd never met, but she hadn't been able to get him out of her mind for the past month.

Gently placing the box in the sand next to her, Whitney opened the envelope with shaking hands and began to read the now-faded letter.

• • •

My Dearest Daughter,

When I chose to become a fireman, I knew this goodbye letter might be necessary one day, even though I always carried my lucky moonstone when I went to fight fires. I wish with all my heart that things were different.

I can picture you growing to look more and more like your mother each day, maybe a little like me too. I hope both are true. I want you to know I fell in love with you the moment your mother told me we were expecting our first child. From that day forward, you became a very special part of my heart and I eagerly anticipated your arrival. There is no doubt in my mind that you will be a blessing in your mother's life, filling her days with joy and happiness.

I want you to have my moonstone and promise me that you will keep it with you at all times. A very unique woman gave it to me claiming it had amazing powers that would keep me from harm. Since I am no longer around to protect you, I must not have heeded her warning. I want you to stay safe, so I urge you to take the powers of this stone seriously.

As I write this, my heart overflows with love for both you and your mother. I am so sorry that I am not with you. Please take good care of each other and treasure the special relationship you have.

Love You Forever,
Dad

• • •

Carefully returning the letter to its envelope, Whitney looked into her mother's tear-filled eyes. Susan brushed a stray hair from her daughter's face. "I have to admit, Whitney, the fact that you're so much like your father has helped me each and every day since his death. It's uncanny how your outlook on life and the way you tackle challenges are so similar. You allow me to feel close to him daily."

"I've kept that letter all these years, waiting for the right time to share it with you. Although there were many times that I was tempted to read it, I never did because your father had written that letter to his daughter, not his wife. I've been concerned that something was upsetting you lately, Whitney, but I felt helpless because I didn't know how to help. That's when I thought of your father's letter, and I hoped he might be able to help you in some way. I was so glad to hear it was exactly all I'd hoped it would be. You just learned how much your father loved you, even before you were born."

"Your timing couldn't have been more perfect, mom. I've been thinking about dad a lot lately. I know it's weird because we never met, but he's been on my mind every day. I just wish his lucky moonstone hadn't failed him. Thank you for sharing my letter tonight, Mom!"

Susan nodded. "I hope you know that you can always come to me when you need to talk, Whitney. You know, from the day I learned your father had been given a lucky moonstone, I noticed he was never without it. He always joked about it being lucky, but I knew deep down he believed in its protective properties."

"I wish I could explain why your father was taken from us, Whitney. It's hard to believe that it's been thirteen years this summer." Sighing softly, Susan quietly added, "Honestly, I have wondered from the time you were born if there was some connection between you and that moonstone. You've always seemed charged with an inner glow and energy, just like your father. Who knows? Maybe there is a little moonlight in you."

"That probably sounds odd coming from your grounded-in-facts mom, but you do seem to possess a special quality. I just wish that you could have met your father and that he could have been here to watch you grow into such a remarkable young lady. You would have loved each other."

"Mom, it just feels like my life is spinning out of control lately. It's like I'm becoming someone different. Does that make any sense? I'm not trying to shut you out of my life when I avoid your questions. Sometimes I just can't find words to explain my thoughts."

"Whitney, the year your father died, I thought the hurt would never go away. Sometimes, I would just sit and stare at you in your crib. You would kick your little legs and turn your head from side to side, taking in your surroundings. And in those moments, I imagined that you were looking for your father. If you hadn't been born the night he died, I honestly don't know if I ever would have recovered from his loss."

They sat quietly, staring into the dying embers, both thinking of the man who was no longer in their lives. It was Susan who broke the silence. "Hey! Why don't you look inside that little box sitting next to you?"

"Oh! I completely forgot!" Whitney eagerly lifted the small box and brushed off the sand. Removing the bow, she unwrapped the paper and opened the lid. Inside, her father's moonstone was nestled in shining iridescent purple paper. "Oh mom, it's so beautiful! But you're giving me dad's moonstone?" She could just picture her father stuffing it into his pocket before he went off to fight fires.

"I certainly am. Your father wanted you to have it. Listen, I was thinking that you and I could go to the jewelry store in town tomorrow so we can have your moonstone made into a necklace."

Holding the stone up to the fire light allowed Whitney to see the intricate designs and patterns on the surface of the stone and the soft lavender colors below the translucent surface. Close to tears, she whispered, "This the nicest thing you've ever done for me, Mom!"

"I'm glad you like it. We should head up to bed now. We have a big day ahead of us tomorrow."

. . .

Hidden in the complete darkness of a lonely beach, the enormous polar bear felt tears roll down her cheeks as she watched mother and daughter walk arm-in-arm up the long flight of stairs. She hadn't expected to hear such an emotional discussion involving Whitney's father's death from thirteen years ago. Her own memories of that horrible night had returned and made her once again face the guilt she'd been living with. Fully aware of how much evil her enemies were capable of, she lived everyday with the terrible realization she should have done more to ensure the safety of Whitney's father.

At the time, Traveller had been certain the deadly storm's chaos and destruction was created by an evil force. She also knew it had been designed to start the fire that took Stan's life. She remembered taking the form of a human to join hundreds of onlookers watching the ravenous fire devour the ten-story apartment building. When she'd learned the devastating news of Stan's death, she'd rushed to the hospital and stood unnoticed in the hallway outside of Susan's room. She was there when Susan received the heartbreaking news. She also discovered the moonstone she'd given him for protection had fallen out of his pocket when he rushed from the truck into the burning building. The mournful sound of Susan's sobs while she held her newborn would stay with her forever.

Susan never knew that her husband had been one of Traveller's chosen ones, so it hadn't occurred to her that her daughter had similar gifts. The danger to Whitney's life was increasing and the nightmares that had started a month ago were only going to worsen, so the bear had travelled back to this world with a very special baby dragon and a plan of action.

This night was far from over, and there was much to be done, but the huge bear smiled through her tears, glad the moonstone was once again right where it belonged. Sitting in the sand preparing for her next move, Traveller sighed under the weight of her heavy burden.

# Chapter Two

# ANOTHER HORRIBLE NIGHTMARE

If Whitney had sensed something magical was about to happen, if she had known that someone powerful and capable of offering explanations was near, her dark mood might have brightened. Her voice might have sounded happier when saying good night to her mother and her steps might have been lighter when walking up to her bedroom.

Crawling into bed, Whitney pulled the comforter up to her chin and pulled Ms. Ellie, her cat, in close. Fearing the return of her terrifying nightmare she tried everything she could think of to stay awake. She read for a while, but that only made her sleepier, so she went to her desk to write to her pen pal, Mallory. When her words became too blurry to continue, she gave up and slipped back into bed.

She was grateful the bonfire had kept her up way past her bedtime. However, she was getting sleepier by the minute and she'd exhausted all of her ideas to stay awake.

Ms. Ellie jumped off the bed as soon as her human fell asleep and leaped onto the window ledge. Staring out into the darkness, she sensed something extraordinary was about to happen. The cat listened to the sound of the waves rolling onto the beach for a short while, but not seeing anything out of the ordinary, she yawned showing big, pointed teeth then returned to bed.

Rudely awakened by Whitney's pitiful moans, Ms. Ellie's concerned eyes watched her. The poor girl was still asleep, but the cat was wide awake and very angry. She knew her young human's terrifying nightmare had returned.

. . .

The mist crept slowly but determinedly through the valley toward her, pausing to investigate every opening in the rocky cliffs surrounding the valley floor. The mountains were high enough to push through the ominous looking clouds overhead that hid the peaks and their inhabitants from view.

Whitney was mesmerized as she watched the mist draw ever closer. Its odd behavior made her think it was looking for something or someone. With a terrifying realization, Whitney began to shake uncontrollably. That mist wasn't looking for just anyone. It was looking for her!

Terrified, Whitney saw shapes inside the mist as it drew closer. Although the shapes were still difficult to identify, she distinctly saw hundreds of bright red eyes. The eerie red glow from all those eyes was intense enough to pierce the mist's dense exterior! She began shivering with fear when she realized they'd discovered her location and were staring right at her. The mist came to a halt not too far from her, and she finally saw the horrid, red-eyed creatures. They lurched out of their transportation in unnatural movements, almost like they'd been forcefully shoved. The mist then moved a short distance away and stopped as if waiting for its passengers to complete a prearranged mission. The ejected creatures didn't move. They just stared at her with undisguised contempt. Why were they so angry with her? What had she done to them?

Whitney covered her eyes to block the horrifying sight, but it was too late. Their frightening images were already imprinted in her brain. Their large, puckered heads were covered in tentacles that moved back and forth in a hypnotic dance. They coiled then struck out like serpents. Their long, distorted fingers ended in sharp curved claws that clicked together threateningly. The deep wrinkled faces of the creatures screamed at her in some foreign language. However, their bright red eyes terrified her the most.

Someone must have given them orders to advance, because all of them began lumbering clumsily toward her at the same time with their clawed fists raised in furious anger. Whitney fearfully watched their approach and wanted desperately to run far away. In horror, she discovered she couldn't move. In fact, it felt like her actions were now being controlled by some invisible force. Feeling utterly helpless, she watched in terror as the hideous creatures moved closer and closer. Who were these creatures anyway, and what was controlling their angry response to her?

They were almost upon her when Whitney heard an ear-piercing shriek from high above. Soon, the lone shriek was joined by many. Looking up, she saw a huge army of dragons soaring down from the mountain peaks, and they were headed toward her. The red-eyed creatures bared their jagged teeth and snarled at the dragons as they approached.

Whitney knew she was no match for the dragons or the mist creatures and felt terribly trapped and very much alone. A sense of doom overtook her, and she called out, "Somebody help! Please!"

Hearing her frantic plea, the lead dragon swooped so low she could see its vivid yellow eyes peering down at her. Unable to look away from the magnificent beast, she blinked in bewilderment. "Had that dragon just smiled at her?" Whitney looked up once again. Still hovering close, the dragon oozed with confidence and winked before soaring skyward to join his army.

Awed by the appearance of such mighty dragons, Whitney was relieved they meant her no harm. In fact, watching their next moves, it appeared they had a common enemy! In a well-practiced maneuver, the mighty dragons extended their huge wings and flew toward

15

the red-eyed mist creatures. Forming a menacing line, they aimed their spiked heads toward the creatures below and unleashed blasts of red-hot fire. Flames landed mere inches from the advancing creatures, which caused a frantic and hasty retreat back into the mist that had rolled in to pick up her passengers. The strange mist wrapped itself around the hideous creatures, cloaked them from sight, then made its way back through the valley.

. . .

Traveller paced back and forth, livid with the creatures terrorizing Whitney. The poor girl had cried out several times in her sleep. Each time, her mom had tiptoed into her daughter's room and sat with her. Gently brushing her hair away from her sweaty forehead, Susan had waited until Whitney's breathing calmed and she'd relaxed again before leaving.

Sensing the girl's torment, the huge bear's anger intensified, and her massive paws carved a deep trench in the sand as she paced. Her enemies had gone too far, and it didn't look like they planned to stop anytime soon. Grateful that the little dragon's father had entered Whitney's dream to reassure the girl when she needed it most, it was now her turn to intervene.

Traveller had skillfully woven a forgetfulness spell into her plan for intervention that would ensure Whitney would remember only that she'd had an amazing dream about a bear and little dragon on her beach. Her magical light show had been carefully designed not only to remove all memories of tonight's nightmare but would also serve to lighten the young girl's heart.

The giant bear looked toward Whitney's window far above her, and whispered soothingly, "Awaken, knowing you have nothing to fear, Whitney. No harm will come to you, of that I can promise. I am very powerful and have never made a promise I can't keep. We will meet soon. When we do, I will explain the reason for your frightening dreams, and other urgent matters. In the meantime, awaken and allow my light to ease your worries."

Whitney woke with a jolt. Her hands were clenched into fists, as she clutched her comforter close to her chin. Confused but curious, she recalled hearing a gentle voice in her dream that had eased her memories of the awful nightmare. Cautiously looking around her room, she could see shadows from a sliver of moonlight through her window, and noticed her cat stretched out on the comforter, grooming herself. Ms. Ellie's bright copper eyes appeared to glow as she stared at Whitney. "I see that voice woke you too, Ms. Ellie."

The light began to grow larger and brighter until it illuminated her entire room. Leaping out of bed, Whitney rushed to the window, and opened it. Amazed at the sight below her, she rubbed her eyes in disbelief, and whispered, "This can't be happening. My eyes must be playing tricks on me!" There was an enormous polar bear looking up at her from the beach far below, surrounded by a bright glow that had to be the source of all of the light. As if that wasn't strange enough, the huge bear talked to her!

"Hello, Whitney! Rest assured your eyes are not playing tricks on you. Allow me to introduce myself. My name is Traveller and I'm from a land called Yagdi."

Distracted by the unbelievable scene below her, Whitney wasn't aware Ms. Ellie had joined her at the window. Perched on the ledge, the cat looked down at the bear, and thought, "It's about time you returned, Traveller! Your guidance has become very much needed."

Raising a monstrous paw, the huge bear took aim and tossed a ball of light high into the air right at Whitney's window saying, "I would like for you to meet my little travelling companion, Aiden. You'll soon see why his name, which means 'Little Fire,' was a perfect choice." Hovering in front of her, the ball of light shattered into millions of colorful diamonds swirling around and around in ever tightening circles. They were so glittery and bright that Whitney had to shield her eyes.

When she removed her hands from her eyes, she was bewildered and amazed to see a tiny dragon floating in the air. Just a few feet away, it was staring at her intensely with huge yellow eyes. "Oh my! You are a 'Little Fire!'" Whitney said softly, "You look just like a tiny version of a huge and magnificent creature from my dream."

The little guy moved his head to the side, grinned, then took off at blinding speed. He became a blur of colorful diamond-shaped scales as he flew excitedly back-and-forth between Whitney and the magnificent bear on the beach below.

Crying out in wonder, Whitney exclaimed, "I can't believe I'm seeing a little dragon. How could that be?" Intrigued by the sound of her voice, Aiden flew closer to investigate this lovely stranger. Guided by an irresistible impulse Whitney stretched her hand out to touch him. When her fingers touched one of his little wings, sparks radiated from her fingertips and flew into the rest of her body. At the same time, as if lightning had struck too close, her hair stood up on her head. Yanking her hand back, Whitney looked at it in shock and mumbled, "What just happened?" Instinctively, the girl didn't fear the strange contact, but knew it had been the result of some kind of powerful attraction between herself and the little dragon.

Temporarily forgotten, relief overwhelmed Traveller, and she smiled at the wonderful sight. The little dragon and Whitney had just made the very powerful connection she'd been hoping for. The girl's joy and wonder were very good signs indeed. Until this moment, the little dragon had never met anyone other than his parents and Traveller. In spite of his limited interactions, he'd apparently realized this girl was very special.

The bear allowed her little friend to fly outside Whitney's

window for quite some time. She noticed Aiden kept returning to Whitney and seemed to enjoy the feel of her touch on his scales. Some of the burden Traveller had been carrying lifted as she looked on with satisfaction and noticed how captivated Whitney was by Aiden. She smiled and thought to herself, "My plan is well on its way. I'm certain those two young ones will become insepa-rable in the very near future."

Finally, the bear nodded her massive head once, signaling for the little dragon to return to the sandy beach. Traveller and Aiden looked up at Whitney and waved. "Goodbye for now," Traveller shouted. "Sleep without fear. Your nightmare will not return tonight dear Whitney." Then, in a flash, they both disappeared.

Although saddened by their sudden departure, Whitney won-dered if she should have been afraid. Staring into the darkness, she murmured, "Did I really just see a glowing polar bear and little dragon? I'll never be able to sleep after that amazing show!" However, before too long, Whitney was surprised to find it had become impossible to resist the urge to sleep.

Scooping her small but surprisingly heavy cat into her arms, she crawled back under her warm comforter and covered them both. Picturing the bear and the little dragon when she closed her eyes, she fell into a deep dreamless sleep within minutes. Ms. Ellie, pressed up against Whitney's back, began to purr contentedly.

• • •

Traveller carried a sleeping little dragon all the way out to Ellie's Point. Very familiar with this narrow strip of land jutting out into Lake Superior, the bear knew it would make an excellent tempo-rary home for the two of them. It was also the perfect location for she and Whitney to meet. The girl walked here often looking for rocks, and Traveller hoped that meeting for the first time in a familiar place would be less threatening.

She soon found the familiar enclosure of huge boulders and towering pine trees that held her portal to Yagdi. It was the perfect spot to keep them hidden from prying eyes. She gently lowered the sleeping dragon onto the bed of soft pine needles covering the sand, and the little guy sighed contentedly in his sleep. Smiling as she turned away, Traveller walked to the very special centuries-old white pine tree growing nearby.

The enormous tree's mighty trunk hid her secret portal that she'd foolishly discarded. She would be needing it once again, so the bear used her unlocking spell. Once that was successfully accomplished, she contacted her friend and teacher, Mergan, on Yagdi. He was happy to hear they'd arrived safely and had connected with Whitney. However, when he asked Traveller whether Whitney would be a good candidate for their very important plan, her honest answer had been that it was too early to tell.

The day had exhausted the bear. As she settled down into the pine needles next to her traveling companion, Traveller considered how best to move forward with Whitney. She had many powers at her disposal, but her ability to transform into a human served her best. It allowed her to blend in quite effectively while on Earth. Confident she'd chosen her first move wisely, the exhausted bear murmured sleepily, "I will become Ursula tomorrow, and I can't wait for us to meet, young Whitney." Daring to hope that today's work had been the dawn of a powerful alliance, the giant polar bear quickly fell asleep.

# Chapter Three

# AN ODD ENCOUNTER

Brilliant sunshine streamed through Whitney's window, urging her to rise and shine. Slowly opening her eyes, she squinted at the bright light. "OK, I get it. I'll get out of bed."

Suddenly Whitney remembered it was the first day of summer vacation. It was also the day her mom was taking her to the jewelry store. She jumped out of bed with a whoop of joy and whistled while she got dressed. Summer was finally here. No more rushing around to catch the school bus that comes way too early. Now she can spend long lazy mornings sleeping in. She can choose to wake up early and watch the sunrise, although she can't see that happening very often, if ever! She can stay in and read by the fire on chilly days, wrapped in a warm blanket. She can stay up late on warm evenings to roast s'mores over a blazing beach bonfire.

She paused to look over at Ms. Ellie who was still in bed. Laughing when her cat stopped grooming to yawn, Whitney teased, "Good Morning, Ms. Ellie. It looks like someone didn't get enough sleep last night! Why might that be? All you have to concern yourself with is your next meal." The cat simply yawned again and eyed Whitney with sweet innocence.

Suddenly hungry for breakfast, a fickle Ms. Ellie stretched one more time, jumped off the bed then ran downstairs. Left alone, Whitney marveled at her cat's never-ending appetite. Pausing to look out her bedroom window before heading downstairs, she gazed at her spectacular view of Lake Superior. "This is going to be the best summer ever!"

Today the visibility was so good she could see the entire length of the peninsula near their house. Sudden movement way out by Ellie's Point caught her eye. "Wow, whatever that is must be huge for me to see it from this distance!"

Raising her window for a better view, sure enough Whitney saw something big and white running near the point. "What on earth is that?" Deciding it would be worthy of further investigation, she ran downstairs to join her mom for breakfast.

Whitney laughed at the sight greeting her in the kitchen. Ms. Ellie was at her food dish, eagerly attacking her breakfast. Holding her tail high and purring loudly, she seemed to be complimenting the chef.

Her mom was standing in front of the stove with her back to Whitney, flipping pancakes. Music always accompanied her mom's cooking and this morning, she was singing, "Our House," one of her favorite "oldies" songs. She'd sung it so often that Whitney knew the words by heart and joined in. Her high soprano voice harmonized well with her mom's deep alto. Any creature swimming, flying or scurrying nearby was sure to hear their enthusiastic voices.

At the sound of her daughter's voice, Susan turned around with a big welcoming smile. "Good Morning! You seem to be in unusually good spirits this morning." Whitney smiled and walked over to kiss her mom's cheek. Smoothing her daughter's hair back, Susan studied her intently. "Are you ready to do a little shopping today?"

Nodding excitedly, Whitney poured their orange juice into small glasses. Remembering the movement out by Ellie's Point, Whitney glanced out the kitchen window. "Hey mom! Come and take a look at this."

At that moment, a seagull glided gracefully past the window. "You called me over to watch a seagull?"

Watching the big bird squawk noisily as it flew gracefully on the wind, she shook her head. "No, not the bird! There's something moving out on Ellie's Point. Look!"

"I don't see anything, Whitney. Now, come and sit down. Breakfast is ready." Carrying a huge pile of pancakes and bacon, Susan placed the platter in front of her daughter. "Ta Da! Here's to the first day of Summer Vacation."

Ms. Ellie, feeling slighted that she was no longer the center of attention, put her nose in the air, raised her tail and walked out of the room in a huff. Whitney and her mom exchanged glances and declared in unison, "There goes Queen Ellie!"

Over blueberry pancakes, they talked excitedly about their trip into town to pick out a chain for Whitney's 'lucky moonstone.'

. . .

Whitney could hardly wait to get to Randolph's Rocks 'N' More Shop. Picking out the perfect necklace for her moonstone would be fun and she really liked the owner, Randolph. Her friend seemed to love his job because he'd been there for over forty years. She always felt welcome because he greeted her with a twinkle in his eyes and a smile that filled his wrinkled face. Sharing her love of rocks, his most treasured display was a case full of cool stones from all over the world. He was always adding to his collection, and she enjoyed listening to the ancient tales about each one. Appreciating her interest, Randolph never missed an opportunity to talk about his collection and would talk for as long as she could stay to listen.

Arriving in town, they parked and walked toward the wooden building that held the rock shop. It looked old and weathered from surviving many long winters on the shore of Lake Superior.

Opening the door, they heard the sound of a little bell somewhere in the back announcing their arrival.

Eager to hear another one of her friend's stories, Whitney led her mom right to Randolph's special collection and waited impatiently for the friendly man to come out of the back room. It was the only clean display in the entire store, which is proof that he considered it special indeed. She could tell that Randolph didn't care much about cleaning, because most of his place hadn't seen a broom or dust cloth in a very long time. She noticed the inside of the shop had the same old feel to it as the outside, with all the discolored and worn log walls. Looking up, she saw spider webs in the beams high above them. Her nose was getting itchy from all the dust, which meant she was going to sneeze any minute. Trying to keep that from happening, she rubbed it while she looked at all the glass cabinets brimming over with amazing stones. Seeing all the stones sparkling with vibrant colors under the bright lights, Whitney was eagerly anticipating her friend's story, and wondered which stone he'd pull out of the case to talk about today.

Instead of her friend, however, an older woman came out of the back room. Patting her hair neatly into place, she wobbled slowly toward the counter where they were standing. Her huge grin created dimples on both of her cheeks, and her eyes twinkled at Whitney's surprised stare, as if she was enjoying a very fun secret. When she reached the counter, she gushed, "My goodness, if it isn't young Whitney and her mother. I'm so excited to finally meet you, young lady. I've been expecting you." Her rough hands looked like they'd seen plenty of hard work, and moved through the air as she talked, as if punctuating every thought.

Noticing how stunned they both looked, she hurried to explain how she knew who they were, when of course neither recognized her. "Ahhh, Randolph has told me all about your love for rocks, Whitney. He says you come in occasionally with your mom to look at our special ones and enjoy hearing tales about a different stone each time. I applaud your interest in rocks." Holding out her hand toward Whitney, she said, "I'm Ursula and I've had that same interest myself for quite a long time."

Seeing this friendly woman smiling at them, they couldn't help but smile back. She was quite short, very plump, and had large twinkling brown eyes. Her eyeglasses looked like they didn't belong on her face but simply sat there as a prop. They stubbornly slid down her long nose to their perch on the end, forcing her to repeatedly push them back up.

Whitney and her mom looked at each other in silent communication. Susan shrugged her shoulders and turned back to face the friendly jeweler. "We've never seen you in here before. It's so nice to meet you, Ursula. I hope Randolph is feeling okay," and shook Ursula's outstretched hand. Ursula smiled again and nodded vigorously, reassuring them that Randolph was indeed fine.

"My daughter wants to see the chains you have for sale. We're interested in having this beautiful moonstone mounted as a necklace. It's a very special stone because it belonged to her father a long time ago."

"Oh, my dear, what a very special treasure that is. May I see your moonstone, young Whitney?" Whitney handed it to Ursula, who once again had to push her glasses back up her long nose. She gazed at Whitney's stone for a very long time. Finally looking up, her eyes held Whitney's. "My young friend, you have a very unique stone indeed. Some say the Moonstone is actually formed by moonlight. They're thought to contain a powerful 'good spirit' within them. It's believed they bring good luck to those who wear them. May I offer you a suggestion?" Ursula asked as she rubbed her hands in gleeful excitement.

Whitney wanted to say yes but looked toward her mom for approval first. When her mom nodded, she answered excitedly, "I'd love to hear your ideas, and maybe a tale or two about your stones, Ursula."

Ursula's hands flew up in delight, then eagerly reached into the case of extra-special stones to pull out two. Whitney could tell they were her favorites, because she placed them so reverently on a black velvet cloth that covered the counter right in front of her. Whitney was instantly captivated by Ursula's tale.

"Your moonstone truly doesn't need anything more. It's a treasure all by itself. However, if you're considering more stones for your new necklace, I think these would complement your beautiful moonstone perfectly. Notice the sparkling quartz on the left. It's so transparent that you can almost see through it." As if in the presence of greatness, she softly explained, "Ancient tales say the crystal quartz holds magic because it was formed long ago from the breath of the White Dragon. It is said that by wearing this stone, a positive energy is released in all directions. It acts as a protector."

Becoming more and more animated as she shared her knowledge, Ursula continued. "Now the one on the right is a very rare and very old Lake Superior Agate, Whitney. Randolph told me that Agates are one of your favorite stones, and there's a good reason they should be. They're extremely special. Do you see the white 'eye' in this particular agate? That 'eye' indicates how rare it is. As you're well aware, our Lake Superior agates can be over a billion years old, which makes them some of the oldest stones on earth. Like the quartz and moonstone, they also have magic to share when the need arises. Very old stories, passed from generation to generation, tell how the 'eye' agate is able to detect evil and will find a way to warn the person wearing it."

"And here's another bit of folklore you may find intriguing. Those known to have special gifts describe feeling a very powerful energy coming from these three stones when they hold them. To everyone else, they simply feel like smooth stones. I found these tales to be so interesting, I actually researched this topic quite thoroughly. Written testimonies actually exist. People claim they've been protected from harm while wearing these stones together.

Ursula rubbed her hands together excitedly and winked, adding, "There won't be an extra charge for these two stones if you choose to add them to your moonstone necklace. Just pick your chain and I'll have your necklace ready for you later this morning. Perhaps you and your mom could find something to do for an hour or so while you're in town. I'll have your necklace in this pretty little box, ready for you when you return." She winked again and said, "Remember, no extra charge."

Whitney and her mom looked at each other once again, something they'd done a lot this strange morning. When her mother smiled and nodded her approval, Whitney turned to the knowledgeable jeweler, "I think the two stones are perfect with my moonstone, and I can't wait to see if I feel their warmth!"

When Ursula took the chosen stones off the counter, Susan announced, "We do expect to pay for them, however." Ursula began to refuse, but Susan raised her hand to stop her, "I don't want to hear anything more about no charge, Ursula. It's very kind, but really not necessary. Let's have Whitney select a chain for her three stones, then she and I will go for some ice cream while we wait for you to create the necklace. When you're finished, please calculate the total, including the extra stones, and have the bill ready when we return. Will an hour be enough time for you?"

Ursula just grinned, pushed her troublesome glasses back into place and assured Susan that one hour would be plenty of time, then reached into the case that held the chains. Pulling out three, she placed one gold chain, one silver chain, and a deep warm brown leather cord on the counter.

Whitney liked them all, but she studied and tested each clasp carefully. Her father's moonstone was so special to her, she wanted to choose a clasp that would be very secure. The lovely leather cord had a clasp that was buffed to a shine you could see yourself in and appeared to be the strongest. Handing that one to Ursula, Whitney said, "This one seems perfect for my three special stones." Taking it from Whitney, Ursula placed it on the counter next to Whitney's three stones, then grinned and said, "Bravo, Young Whitney. Excellent choice!"

As they left the store, Susan and Whitney linked arms and turned toward the Sweet Shoppe just two blocks away. Ursula opened the jewelry store windows to let the lovely lake breeze in and grinned at the mother and daughter walking away smiling and chatting like two best friends. Preparing to turn away, she was surprised to see them both stop abruptly and turn to stare at each other with identical expressions of bewilderment. Curious over their unexpected behavior, she moved closer to the window and waited long enough to hear Susan ask her daughter, "I know it was almost five years ago, and you were only eight years old, but doesn't Ursula remind you of the woman we bought our house from?" Whitney was stunned at her mom's question because she'd just been thinking the same thing. With no way to explain this strange phenomenon, they just shook their heads and laughed. Ursula laughed too and returned to the counter. "If they only knew the accuracy of their innocent observation!"

Still grinning, Ursula polished Whitney's very powerful stones with a special cloth then strung them onto the charmed cord. She wrote a hurried note and placed it with the necklace into a drawer marked "completed orders," then left the store.

Whitney and her mom wandered slowly down River Street, stopping occasionally to gaze at attractive shop displays. When they arrived at the Sweet Shoppe, they both ordered two scoops of ice cream in waffle cones. Whitney asked for chocolate on chocolate topped with colorful sprinkles, her absolute favorite, while Susan wanted to taste the flavors of coconut and fresh strawberries. Knowing they still had an hour to wait, they savored their treats, down to the last crumb of cone and lick of ice cream, before they licked their sticky fingers.

They sighed contentedly and sat back in their seats to enjoy the sun's warmth and each other's company. Preoccupied, they failed to notice the woman across the street who watched them so intently. She smiled when they laughed and appeared to enjoy the scene immensely.

Undetected, Ursula watched them finish their ice cream then walk slowly back to the jewelry store. With a grin on her face, she whispered, "I can't wait for you to pick up the necklace I designed just for you, young Whitney. It'll be so much fun to watch your reaction to the stones' energy when you put the necklace on."

# Chapter Four

# A MYSTERIOUS DISAPPEARANCE

Opening the door to the jewelry store, they once again heard the bell announce their presence. Whitney was excited to see what Ursula has created for her. However, it wasn't the elderly woman who walked through the back door.

Whitney was surprised to see her jeweler friend, Randolph, come out. Walking up to the counter, he smiled warmly and greeted Susan, then turned to Whitney, "Welcome back! I've missed you. Maybe now that school's out for the summer I'll see more of you and your mom. Shall we pull out a special stone so I can tell you it's story?"

Stunned at this unexpected turn of events, and thinking he may be a little confused, Susan gently explained, "We were actually here just an hour ago, and there was another person standing right where you are now. I assumed she was assisting you."

Noticing her words had truly stunned the shop owner, Susan gently continued, "The woman we just spoke with said her name was Ursula. She appeared to be an avid rockhound, just like you and my daughter. She helped Whitney pick out two stones to compliment the moonstone. She even took the time to share the folklore surrounding each stone, just as you like to do."

The poor store owner stood speechless, scratching his head and looking horribly confused. Finding his voice, Randolph admitted, "This is strange indeed. I actually just opened my shop a few minutes ago. It was closed all morning because I had business to attend to. I don't know of anyone named Ursula. I do hire a woman to come in and help when I get busy, but her name isn't Ursula."

Just then, Randolph appeared to remember something that may shed some light on this mystery. "How on earth could I have forgotten? I did have an assistant by the name of Ursula, but only for a very short while. I want to say it was at least three or four years ago now. She left town about the same time you both moved into your home. I can't imagine that same woman would have broken into my shop this morning and sold you a necklace, for heaven's sake!"

Whitney and Susan appeared startled by his revelation. This sweet man seemed genuinely caught off guard and looked like he wanted so badly to make sense of this situation. Susan offered a suggestion. "The woman we just saw in here was going to have the necklace ready for us today, along with the bill. Can you just look under the counter to see if there's a little box with a brown leather necklace and three stones inside? It would be under my name."

Still baffled, Randolph shook his head and bent down. Pulling out a drawer labeled "completed orders" they heard him mumble, "Well I'll be." Rising, he placed a little black box on the counter in front of them. Looking right at Susan, he said, "I'm certainly mystified. However, I assure you I will get to the bottom of this. As soon as I find out anything more about your mysterious Ursula, I'll let you know."

Opening the box, he pulled out Whitney's necklace and gaped at its beauty. He looked from the necklace to Whitney and her mom and said softly, "This is a spectacular necklace indeed! You say this Ursula told you the significance of each, eh? Did she also tell you how powerful the three can be when put together?" When they nodded, he placed the necklace into Whitney's hands.

She immediately felt the warmth from the stones, as if she'd just pulled them out of the sand on a hot summer day. It felt weird, but not threatening. Staring at her necklace, Whitney wondered what was causing the warmth and why the jeweler hadn't mentioned it.

Peeking through the grimy jewelry store window, Ursula watched eagerly as Randolph brought out the necklace. As soon as it was placed in the girl's hand, Ursula knew Whitney had indeed felt the warmth from the stones. With a huge grin, she took her irritating glasses off and said, "Ahh, just as I suspected, young chosen one. That necklace is right where it's meant to be. I'm truly looking forward to a very long friendship, and I'm confident you'll learn quickly and rise to the challenges you will soon be experiencing. It's time we met, Whitney. See you at Ellie's Point tomorrow."

Turning away with an excited grin, Ursula headed toward the deserted beach just a few blocks away. Looking in every direction to make sure there were no prying eyes, she began to walk more quickly than someone might expect of an elderly woman. As she walked, she grew taller and more muscular, then suddenly transformed into a magnificent bear. Her movements became swift and sure as her powerful leg muscles propelled her away from town and out toward Ellie's point.

Removing the necklace from her daughter's hands, Susan took her daughter's shoulders, gently turned her around and placed it around her neck, making sure the shiny clasp closed completely. Then, just to make sure it was good and tight, she tried to unclasp it, but it wouldn't budge. Puzzled, she asked the jeweler to try taking it off. He was no more successful than Susan. Completely baffled, all Randolph could say was, "Huh! Now that's odd. Whitney, we've tried our darnedest. You give it a try."

To their surprise, the clasp opened easily for Whitney. Mystified, she asked the store owner, "What's going on? How can I unclasp it when neither of you can?" Poor Randolph reached for

the necklace, knowing there had to be an answer to this strange phenomenon. Feeling sorry for the puzzled jeweler, Whitney put the necklace into his hand and watched him put on his spectacles. Then he pulled out a huge magnifying glass for an even closer look at the clasp. Susan moved in to look over his shoulder and both peered at it through the high-powered magnifying lens.

Whitney began to miss the warmth from the stones and grew increasingly impatient with their methodical inspection. When Randolph finally handed it back to her, she quickly put it back on. Securing the clasp, she felt the warmth once again and sighed in contentment. That's when she noticed the baffled look on both of their faces, mixed with a little concern. Running his hand through his rumpled hair, the jeweler shook his head. "As much as I wish I had an answer to this strange circumstance, I don't have a clue why Whitney is the only one who can open this clasp."

"When I chose the leather cord with that cool looking clasp, I told myself I wanted a necklace that no one could take off but me," Whitney spoke softly, as if disclosing a secret. "I guess that leather necklace and its clasp took me literally!" She gave a light-hearted laugh, but it came out pretty lame and she could see they weren't buying her explanation for one second.

Susan and Randolph simply shrugged their shoulders. "As long as Whitney can remove it when she wants to, that's good enough for the time being. We'll take it, Randolph. Can you show us the bill so we can pay you?" Obviously still confused, he scratched his head yet again and mumbled something to himself as he opened the drawer and found the bill. With a puzzled expression, Randolph looked at Susan and chuckled, "Well, this day is certainly full of surprises!" and showed it to Susan. Scrawled across the top in big bold letters were two words: 'No Charge!'

35

Shaking her head, Susan started to argue, "We can't leave without paying you for these stones and lovely necklace. Please tell me its value." Randolph thought for a moment and Whitney saw his expression turn from mystified to good-humored then he laughed. "If that's the worst thing that happens to me this week, I'll consider myself a lucky man. Whitney loves her rocks as much as I do. It will be an honor to see her wearing stones from my shop, especially knowing she appreciates how special they are. Please accept it as my gift and go enjoy the rest of your day." Susan thought about it for a minute. Realizing this sweet man was completely serious, she gave in. "Okay I'll accept that, Randolph, and thank you so very much for encouraging my daughter's interest in stones. We'll be back to shop here often. Whitney loves hearing your mysterious tales about all of the gems and minerals, don't you Whitney?" Whitney smiled broadly and nodded eagerly in agreement, while she fingered her stones on the necklace.

The jeweler looked relieved and said, "It's settled then. Please enjoy wearing that stunning necklace which contains a mystery of its own, Whitney. Come back often. I always look forward to your visits." As Randolph turned to go back to his room hidden behind the curtain, Susan posed one more question. "Did you by chance know the woman we bought our house from?"

Considering Susan's unexpected question for a moment he finally answered, "I remember she seemed like a very mysterious person to all of us. By our town's standards, she didn't live here long, maybe eight years or so. No one knew much about her, as I recall. She always seemed polite enough but wasn't one to socialize. She never took the time to have a friendly conversation with any of us. She came in for supplies, but always left town as soon as her shopping was done. I might add, though, that when she and Ursula both suddenly vanished about four or five years ago, they were the talk of the town for quite some time. Here one day, then mysteriously gone the next. Just like that! Sorry I can't tell you more."

Walking out the door, Whitney laughed, "Well mom it looks like we have another mystery to solve. Do you suppose Ursula the jeweler might be the same woman who sold us her house? I'd love to solve that!" They were both laughing as they waved good-bye to the smiling jeweler and walked out of the store. Shaking her head, Susan said, "I hope Randolph discovers who our mysterious Ursula is very soon, for his sake and ours. I felt sorry for him when we told him about the woman who'd helped us earlier today. He looked so shocked, didn't he? I can't wait to find out who on Earth that woman was, and what she was doing in his store. I'm pretty certain he's feeling the same way!"

Back on the street, Susan suddenly stopped and grabbed Whitney's arm. With a secretive grin on her face, she whispered, "We may be onto something! Wouldn't it be crazy if Ursula and the woman who sold us her house were one and the same? Think about it. They have many of the same mannerisms, and they share similar physical characteristics. But if that's true, don't you think it's odd she didn't recognize us? Even more puzzling, what if she did know who we were, but didn't say anything?" Whitney just shook her head at this odd morning, unable to come up with an answer that made any sense.

On the car ride home, Whitney's mom hummed along with a song on the radio. Whitney looked out the window enjoying the occasional view of Lake Superior gleaming in the sunlight. Feeling the warmth around her neck, she reached up to touch her necklace then frowned. If Ursula's strange tales were true, and that was a big if, then that meant she must possess special gifts. Could that have something to do with the disquieting thoughts she's been experiencing recently?

# Chapter Five

# LETTER FROM A FRIEND

Whitney stretched then grinned as she touched her necklace. "Hmmm, I wonder if the stones were responsible for such a peaceful night's sleep." Shrugging her shoulders, she threw off her covers and walked over to the window. Certain she'd just seen movement, she murmured, "Oh no, not again!" However, when she looked once more, she didn't see anything out of the ordinary. "There wasn't anything out there to be afraid of! It was just my eyes playing tricks on me again." A little disappointed, Whitney admitted the possibility of something big and white running way out there at the end of the peninsula caused her to shiver with excitement. "I'll be extra vigilant today, just in case."

The warm breeze and sunlight coming through her window promised it would be a beautiful summer day for collecting stones and driftwood on the beach. She threw on a pair of bright green shorts, a green striped t-shirt and flip-flops, and once again touched her new necklace. Feeling a little silly, Whitney realized she wasn't ready to share its existence with anyone but her mom and tucked it protectively under her T-shirt. Then, grabbing her beach bag, Whitney hurried downstairs. Susan was nowhere in sight, but she'd left a pile of mail on the counter. Right on the top was a letter addressed to her. Seeing New Zealand on the envelope, she ripped it open to read her pen pal's letter.

• • •

Dear Whitney,

All is well here. My family's heading up into the mountains to camp this weekend. Of course, our campsite has to be by a trout stream so dad can fish, and near a mountain bike trail for Edward to ride. Speaking of Edward, I've been living with a very grumpy twin brother this past month. He's no fun because he's moody all the time. I'm tired of grumpy. I want my fun brother back. I try to help, but when I ask him what's going on, he just mumbles that I wouldn't understand. He says he'll deal with it himself, then walks away. I feel bad for him, and wish he'd tell me what's going on, but he just keeps pushing me away.

Enough of that. Are you ready for really big news? I'm very jealous of my brother because he gets to do something I've been wanting to do since we became pen pals. Edward's coming to Michigan in a week! He'll be staying with grandma and grandpa, right down the beach from you!!! Why does he always get to do the cool stuff? Maybe being grumpy gets rewarded. So totally not fair!! I should work on perfecting my grumpy side. Then maybe I'd be the one going to Michigan to see you instead of Edward!

Still, I'm really excited for him. A few months ago, he read about a world-wide Mountain Bike Competition to be held in Michigan in late summer. He submitted his application and waited months for a response. Needless to say, that didn't help his mood at all! Just yesterday he finally got the good news he was accepted. The events coordinator told him that he was one lucky kid because this was the first time in ten years some-one had canceled at the last minute.

Anyway, it'll be held at a place called Iron Mountain in the Porcupine Mountains close to you and your mom. Have you been there? The pictures of all the pine trees and lakes look awesome! It's a triath-lon, so he has to train for three events: running, swimming and biking. Sounds gruesome to me, but he's thrilled and excited to start training. He's been given "Number 51." Now he's finding anything that has the number 51 on it, cutting it out and adding it to his growing collection, which is quickly taking over his bedroom walls. Guess he's a little excited, right?

He'll be leaving right after our family camping trip and arriving at grandma and grandpa's trailer next week…lucky him!!!!! When my grandparents found out Edward would be with them for the whole sum-mer, they said they were 'tickled pink.' Their expres-sions crack me up! Anyway, in a rare moment of cell service, I looked on Google Earth, and found the Hiawatha National Forest campground where they're hosts. It looks like you can easily walk to it from your house.

I wish it was me, Whitney!!! Mom and dad said some-day I'll get to do the same thing…but probably not this summer! Poor me!! They didn't say I absolutely wasn't coming, so I'm still holding onto the very slim possibility. Keep your fingers and toes crossed for me.

Grandma and grandpa will be getting in touch with you and your mom so you and my brother can meet. Ugh! I don't think you'll like him much. When you named him 'biker dude' last year, you described him perfectly. He just wants to ride his silly mountain bike all the time, so I don't think you'll have much in common. Believe me, all he'll talk about is mountain biking or his competition. It'll bore you to death!!! Unfortunately, you'll probably see a lot of each other because he'll be running the beach, swimming and riding biking trails to train for the 'Big Competition.' All I can say is good luck with him! I hope you can figure out how to avoid him. That's just a small warning from your best pen pal friend.

I have to cut this short and finish packing for the trip into the mountains. By the time you get this, Edward may already be there, and my grandparents will be calling your mom. Sorry I couldn't give you a heads-up sooner than this. Please write soon. I can't wait to hear how your first meet-up goes!

Love,

Mallory

• • •

Staring at her pen pal's letter, Whitney was baffled by this new development. Chewing on her thumbnail, she considered what Mallory had said about her brother. It sure sounded like he was going to be difficult to like. She'd been looking forward to a nice long summer, doing exactly what she wanted to do. That's what summers are for, right? Babysitting her friend's biker brother simply didn't fit into those plans. Mallory's grandparents and Edward could be planning a get together at this very moment. Working herself into a worried mess, Whitney took a deep breath and put the letter down. "Time for a quick breakfast and a walk on the beach. That'll calm my nerves."

Just then, she heard the telephone ring and Susan's muffled voice coming from her office. "Well hello to you too. This is a pleasant surprise. Yes, Thursday would be wonderful. How about coming over for a cookout? We can grill hamburgers. Yes, your beans and potato salad sound wonderful. Excellent! See you soon." Then her mom called out, "Whitney! Are you in the kitchen? Wait right there. I have a surprise for you."

# Chapter Six

## ELLIE'S POINT

Walking into the kitchen with a huge grin, Susan looked at her daughter excitedly. "I just spoke with your pen pal's grandma and guess what she told me. Oh, never mind, I won't make you guess because you couldn't, not in a million years! Mallory's brother Edward just arrived. He's staying with them at the campground down the beach all summer so he can train for some biking competition at Iron Mountain. I just invited them over for a Bar-B-Q on Thursday."

The cereal in her mouth was suddenly terribly dry. Choking it down, Whitney blurted out, "You've got to be kidding me!" Her poor mom's smile immediately turned into a frown, so she quickly explained, "Mom, this party could be a disaster! I just read Mallory's letter and she told me that her brother was coming. Her advice was, 'Good luck with my brother!' Ugh, mom, I wish they weren't coming over at all."

Susan's face turned from puzzled to sympathetic. She'd intended to tease her daughter that a boy was coming over but wisely decided it wasn't such a good idea. "I've already committed us, so how about we play nice because it's the polite thing to do. We can welcome him to the area and never have to plan any other get togethers. His grandma just explained he's going to be very busy training for his competition in a couple of months anyway. Who knows? He may turn out to be nicer than Mallory described. Keep in mind she might have a somewhat slanted view because she's his sister. Anyway, Mallory's grandparents are the ones who encouraged you and Mallory to become pen pals, so we owe them a thank you for that, right?"

"You're right. I can use the opportunity to get them caught up on what Mallory's up to. She's a great long-distance friend now!"

Relieved, Susan headed toward the clinic. "Good luck finding rocks today. I hope an agate winks up at you!"

Whitney made tuna sandwiches, spread peanut butter on crackers, grabbed a handful of Oreo cookies, then filled a jug with water. Stuffing her bag with her lunch, a towel, sunscreen and some small baggies for cool beach finds, she walked to the door. Excited to be off on another adventure, Ms. Ellie almost tripped Whitney several times as they headed down the steep wooden stairway to the beach.

When they reached the beach, Whitney looked in the direction of Ellie's Point a mile away. The image of something huge returned and sent excited shivers through her. "Is there something out there I should fear?"

The peninsula ending at Ellie's Point reached so far over the deep cold waters of Lake Superior, it had always seemed full of mystery and secrets to Whitney. When dense fog rolled in and cloaked the shoreline, it became even more mysterious. During those dark foggy nights, she'd hear the eerie sound of foghorns from nearby lighthouses warning ships and their crews of dangers ahead. Like a stubborn child, the dense fog worked equally hard to muffle those warning sounds.

Ships moved invisibly through the fog and answered with their own sounds of warning. Their captains, well aware of the dangerous obstacles near the end of the point, always took extra precautions. They'd blast their ships' horns frequently as they moved slowly and cautiously forward, informing other ships of their location.

Whitney looked at her feline companion, shrugged her shoulders and with a slight quiver in her voice announced, "It's a beautiful day, with no clouds or fog on the horizon. Come on, girl, let's race to the point."

Ms. Ellie raced away and was soon out of sight. "I should've known she'd leave me behind! Sometimes, my dear little cat doesn't behave like a cat at all, but more like the wild cats on the nature shows I love to watch." Certain she'd catch up with Ms. Ellie eventually, Whitney moved slowly toward the point. Her attention turned excitedly toward the line of rocks pushed onto the beach along the shoreline. The farther she walked, the calmer she became. Lake Superior had always had that effect on her. So far, there had been no strange sightings, but no sign of Ms. Ellie either.

Try as she might, she couldn't stop thinking of Mallory's warning and dreaded the thought of meeting her brother. "Man, what a way to ruin a perfectly good day." A couple of summers ago, Mallory's grandparents had been hired as camp hosts in the National Forest campground near Whitney's house. They'd met one day walking on the beach and discovered they all enjoyed looking for rocks, especially agates. She'd liked both of them instantly, and they'd become great friends.

On one of their walks, Mallory's grandmother had suggested Whitney and her granddaughter become Pen Pals. She explained sadly that Mallory's family lived in New Zealand, and she and her husband missed them terribly. They were so far away and staying in touch was difficult because their internet and phone service was very unreliable. Then she'd pointed out that Whitney and her granddaughter were close to the same age, so she just knew they'd have a lot to talk about.

Not wanting to disappoint her new friend, Whitney had agreed to give it a try. She soon realized that writing letters by hand was far from the burden she'd expected. In fact, she kind of enjoyed putting her thoughts down on paper. Whitney discovered Mallory's grandma was right. They did have a lot in common. They tried to write every month and looked forward to hearing about each other's new adventures.

Mallory wrote about her brother, Edward, a lot. Whitney knew he was an avid mountain biker always looking for adventurous rides into the mountains and following riverbeds. He was on his school's biking team and they'd won many awards.

Whitney finally stopped daydreaming and looked up. Surprised to see how close she was to the point the bright sunlight made her squint as she turned in a circle looking for her cat. No Ms. Ellie in sight. However, there was a large mound of sugar-white sand not too far away that she'd never seen before. "Hmmm, I wonder what brought that to my beach. It certainly looks worthy of investigation."

Suddenly the huge sand pile moved just a little. Whitney stopped and stared, suddenly remembering the huge white creature she thought she'd seen from her bedroom window. Running a shaking hand through her hair, she tried to convince herself everything was all right. "There's nothing to fear. I have my necklace on and Ursula said my stones would warn me if danger was near." It worked to restore her confidence, but she still moved forward more slowly and with extreme caution. In fact, the closer she got to the mysterious mound, the more uncomfortable she became.

She was almost to the mound when it moved slightly then rose high into the air. Bringing her hands to her mouth, Whitney gasped in terror at the sight. The large mound wasn't sand at all! Looming over her, and far too close, was a giant polar bear at least three times her height. Even more shocking, right next to the beast was her cat, grooming herself as if she didn't have a care in the world!

Whitney, on the other hand, cared a great deal! Frozen with fear, she gaped helplessly at the bear. Finding her voice, she shouted, "Move! Come here Ms. Ellie! We need to get out of here!'" She moved toward her cat intending to grab her, but in dismay realized she didn't have time to save them both.

With her eyes focused on the bear Whitney inched slowly backward, turned around and in a panic broke into a run. Stumbling on a rock, she twisted her ankle and lost her balance. As if in slow motion, she watched the sand rise to meet her face and landed hard. Feeling excruciating pain radiating from her ankle, Whitney gasped, "Ouch, my ankle!" Then she turned onto her back and spit out a mouthful of sand.

With lightning speed, Ms. Ellie took one giant leap, and landed on top of Whitney. In spite of the horrible pain, she couldn't hold back the giggle as her cat's whiskers tickled her face. Satisfied Whitney would be all right, the cat settled into the sand at her shoulder.

Grateful that her cat appeared to be safe, Whitney felt beyond frightened. Not knowing what else to do, she looked up at the bear standing over her and began screaming in a high-pitched wail, "Who are you anyway? What are you doing on my beach? How did you get here? Everyone knows you can't talk to bears, so why am I? Why do you seem so familiar? Are you the same bear I saw with a little dragon in my dream?"

Thinking this impossible mess couldn't get any crazier, two big yellow eyes suddenly peered out from between the bear's monstrous front paws. Shocked speechless, Whitney stared at the bear and whatever was hiding under her. Adding to her confusion, Ms. Ellie began to purr! At a loss for what to think or do next, Whitney cried, "It's Official! I've lost my mind!"

It pained the baby dragon to hear such distress in the girl's voice. He wanted desperately to comfort her but had promised Traveller he'd stay hidden behind her. However, this girl sounded

so sad, he just had to look. Barely the size of a squirrel, the tiny dragon had a difficult time seeing around the huge bear, even when he stretched his little body as far as it could go. If he remained behind the monstrous bear, he'd never see her.

Unable to restrain himself any longer, he quickly crawled toward the bear's front paws. His heart wasn't prepared for the scene before him, and the little dragon felt a salty tear fall down his cheek. There was a poor girl laying in the sand, and she was crying! He now understood what his mother had meant when she'd explained their big dragon hearts cared deeply about others. It was this compassion that made them the perfect protectors of Yagdi. He was feeling, for the first time in his young life, how much it hurt to care so deeply.

Whitney knew she was in a no-win situation and had apparently lost her sanity. Gathering her last ounce of courage, she sat up and squared her shoulders. Looking the bear right in the eye, she announced in a shaky voice, "This is beyond my comprehension! I'm scared to death and I can't run away. I'm going to get up now and limp home. If you intend to make me your lunch, there's nothing I can do about it."

Hearing the distress in the poor girl's voice, the impatient little dragon was unable to wait another second. Blinking his tears away, he raced to Whitney, leaped into her arms, and bathed her face tenderly with his huge tongue. Caught off guard, Whitney fell backward and landed on top of Ms. Ellie, which caused the cat to spring to her feet and yowl in surprise. In an attempt to preserve her dignity, the cat sat down and began to groom, as if that had been her intent all along.

The little dragon, however, thought this was some kind of delightful new game. Excited, he jumped up and began chasing his tale, returning again and again to lick Whitney's face. Deciding her little friend was having too much fun without her,

Ms. Ellie began to chase him in dizzying circles, with Whitney in the middle.

Blaming her next action on temporary insanity, Whitney did something that surprised even herself. Grinning at the little dragon, she opened her arms. The baby dragon was so happy to see her smile he raced into her outstretched arms, snuggled close and released a contented sigh.

When Whitney looked up, the huge bear was smiling at her, so she relaxed just a little bit. Thinking she was talking to herself, she mused, "How on Earth did you and a little dragon end up on my beach?" When the bear answered her, Whitney's fear rushed back!

Adeptly seizing this opportunity, Traveller answered, "Young Whitney, meet Aiden. His name was chosen at birth by his parents and means Little Fire. Appropriate name for a dragon, don't you agree?" Chuckling at her own joke, the polar bear moved just a little closer to inspect the girl's injury. "That ankle looks too sore to move, at least for the time being."

Whitney stared at the talking polar bear, then looked down at the little dragon in her arms. She tried hard to steady her voice, but her teeth still chattered, "Big huge polar bears don't talk to humans, especially not in a grandma voice. And how can you possibly know my name?"

The bear's big brown eyes twinkled with a mixture of concern and amusement. Leaning in closer, she said gently, "I'm going to sit down next to you, but please don't fear me. I promise I won't think of lunch, or any meal for that matter, when I look at you. I just want to stay with you until your ankle feels better."

Settling in the sand, the bear looked at the little dragon on Whitney's lap. "Why don't you and Ms. Ellie run off and have some fun while Whitney and I get to know each other?" Aiden smiled his big goofy grin then jumped off Whitney's lap to race away with Ms. Ellie in close pursuit. Watching the little dragon run off with her cat, Whitney was surprised at how fond she'd become of 'Little Fire' in such a short period of time and murmured, "He's so irresistibly cute!" She was now very much alone and sitting very close to a huge talking polar bear. "I really should be more afraid of you, but for some reason I'm not! How strange this day is turning out to be!" Then she looked right at the bear sitting next to her and continued, "People who talk to each other should use their names. You seem to know mine, so what should I call you?"

"You can call me Traveller."

Whitney remained in disbelief but no longer felt the least bit threatened. Curiosity had gotten the best of her, and she was intrigued by the bear's sly grin and eyes full of mischief and mystery. In fact, at the moment she couldn't think of anything more interesting than hanging out for the day on the shores of Lake Superior with this unique bear and little dragon.

"I never thought this day would bring a talking polar bear and dragon into my life, and I can't wait to see what happens next."

Whitney's admission was wonderful to hear. Relieved the tricky introductions were behind them, Traveller closed her eyes and tipped her face toward the sun. She knew the girl was watching her with keen interest, but the bear didn't want to push things too quickly, so she remained silent.

Whitney was indeed watching the sunlight turn the magnificent bear's thick fur into an amazing rainbow of moving, shimmering colors. She shivered as she suddenly remembered a bear in her recent nightmare. It had looked identical to the bear now sitting so close to her.

# Chapter Seven

# TRAVELLERS REST

Whitney sighed as the soothing warmth from the sun and the sound of gentle waves began to ease her fears. She and Traveller sat in comfortable silence, enjoying the entertainment a large group of seagulls were providing. Perpetually hungry, the gulls darted in and out of the water in their never-ending search for food. When a fish was caught, their squawking became feverish as they all flew excitedly toward the catch. Whitney snuck frequent glances at the bear and noticed her new friend's mouth would water each time one of the seagulls caught a fish.

Nervous that she was sitting so close to a hungry bear, Whitney decided it was time to share her lunch, so she reached into her bag. Grabbing the food, she put it on her towel. Ms. Ellie and Aiden appeared out of nowhere and took a seat near the food and stared at it intently. She knew that look because she'd seen it often in her cat. They were hoping for a handout. It's a good thing she'd packed tons of food and cat treats. Aiden soon discovered he liked cat treats, and eagerly took each one she offered, then begged for more.

She shared the rest of her lunch with the polar bear, who finished all too quickly. Watching Traveller lick every morsel of tuna fish off her long claws, she hoped the big bear had gotten enough to eat. Even the Oreo cookies were gone in seconds. Smiling at Whitney, the bear burped and declared, "What a lovely snack. Thank you, young Whitney!"

After lunch, the cat and dragon curled up beside Whitney and promptly fell fast asleep. Petting each of them, Whitney gazed out over the water, mulling over the sight of the bear and Ms. Ellie when she'd first walked up. Seeing them sitting together like long-lost friends made her wonder if they'd met before today.

Whitney soon discovered that her new friend was a very interested listener and felt encouraged to share stories about her life. Oddly, her friend seemed to be the most interested in her house, so Whitney used great detail when she explained how they'd found it, and why it was so perfect for them. She told the bear that her mom was a vet and had always dreamed of having her own practice out of their home.

"That meant it had to be pretty large. We looked a long time for the right house, and almost gave up many times. We'd gotten pretty discouraged and wondered if our 'perfect house' just didn't exist when one day, we saw a 'For Sale' sign, almost covered up with weeds. When we knocked, a sweet older woman came to the door and seemed quite happy to see us. We loved the house from the moment we walked in and bought it that day. It's completely surrounded by Lake Superior to the north and the National Forest nearby, so we have the space, beauty, peace and quiet we both enjoy."

"I'm so glad you and your mom are happy living there. It's a very special house and location indeed!"

Whitney wondered how the bear knew so much about their house. "Your name reminds me of the elderly lady who sold us her home. She called it 'Travelers Rest,' just like your name. Strange as it sounds, you and she have very similar mannerisms. Of course, that can't be possible with a human and a polar bear, but what an interesting coincidence!"

Noticing Traveller's eyes gleamed with a sudden intensity, she continued, "Anyway, we thought it sounded so welcoming that mom engraved the name onto a sign outside the entrance to her clinic's door."

Traveller's huge grin made Whitney say, "I really have to remember who you remind me of!"

After carrying on for quite some time, Whitney realized she hadn't given her friend the opportunity to talk about herself. There was just something about the bear that made her want to share everything. Her friend clearly enjoyed hearing about Whitney's life because she asked many questions and nodded her head often.

When Whitney asked her about life in the arctic, it made the bear pause. She wasn't sure how much she wanted to divulge in one day. She wanted Whitney to know she and Aiden were from a different world, a land far away called Yagdi. The girl would soon learn the bear was on a mission that involved her. However, she still needed time to build Whitney's trust, so she decided her news could wait a day or two. She would just have to play the role of an Earthly polar bear for a little while longer.

Having done some research on Earth's polar bears, Traveller eagerly shared what she'd read about the cold northern arctic, and hoped it sounded believable. Warming up to the challenge, the bear captivated Whitney as she explained how important her thick coat of fur was. She had to swim through the frigid waters from one iceberg to the next in search of food and relied on her fur to keep her warm. Whitney loved nothing more than out-door adventures and listened attentively. Traveller promised that Whitney could visit her home one day.

After a beautiful day of sunshine and wispy clouds, the after-noon shadows began to lengthen. Whitney repositioned herself, which prompted the polar bear to ask, "How is that ankle of yours feeling?"

"I think the swelling is going down, but I don't think I'm ready to stand on it just yet."

Traveller rubbed her jaw and gazed out across the lake, as she weighed her next move very carefully. Noticing the bear's pensive mood, Whitney asked, "Is there something on your mind?"

Dropping her paw, Traveller looked at her young friend. "Yes, there is, Whitney. Can you tell me about your bad dreams?"

Taken completely by surprise, Whitney stared at the bear then shook her head admitting, "I'd hoped shocking revelations were over for the day. Not so lucky, I guess. I can't believe you know about my nightmares and I want to hear more about that. However, to answer your question, yes, I've been terrified by nightmares for a month now. I dread them so much I'm afraid to fall asleep!"

The bear nodded and asked encouragingly, "Can you tell me about them?"

"Before I do, please tell me how on earth you knew about my nightmares?" Whitney blurted.

"I know many things and have been watching over your family since before you were born."

Growing more upset, Whitney demanded, "You knew my dad too?"

"I did, and I know you and your father have a great deal in common. You were both born with extraordinary gifts. Your father wasn't aware of his, and neither are you. Not yet anyway."

It was difficult to cope with this incredible news and Whitney felt an uncomfortable mix of excitement and bewilderment. "I can't believe you know about my nightmares, and you knew my dad! How? You have to tell me!"

"I gave your father his moonstone, Whitney. I was in Chicago watching over him for the same reason I'm with you now. You are in danger and I've come to protect you."

Fully aware of just how much she was asking of this brave young girl, the bear simply sat and waited for Whitney's outburst. Sure enough, a few seconds later Whitney jumped up, but winced from the sharp pain in her ankle and had to sit right back down. Terribly overwhelmed, she yelled in a strangled voice, "I can't believe you knew my father, and you were the one who gave him his so-called protective moonstone. How can you say you'd protect me, when you couldn't protect my dad?"

Traveller's expression suddenly reflected overwhelming sadness, which made Whitney wish she hadn't said such harsh words. "Traveller, I never should have..."

The bear broke her off, and said quietly, "That was a fair question, Whitney. While I was watching your father, our enemy was becoming increasingly stronger. Unfortunately, I wasn't aware of that at the time. I still feel responsible for your father's death because I could have prevented it had I been more vigilant. I should have known what our enemy was up to."

Traveller looked sadly at the young chosen one and said tenderly, "I know you're struggling with this information, so I have a suggestion. Why don't we part ways for today, and plan to meet here again tomorrow? You need time to think about what you've just heard. I'm sure that you'll return with many questions for me and I promise to be completely honest with my answers. With the help of a fresh new day, we can tackle all of it together."

Although she was reluctant to say good-bye to her friend, Whitney had been gone a long time. Shrugging her shoulders, she agreed, "Okay, I'll be here again tomorrow." With a weak grin, she added, "And you're right, I've already got a few questions in mind."

The bear rose and stretched, "Of course you do. I wouldn't expect any less from you, young Whitney. By the way, I'm quite certain one of your gifts is tenacity. You have a questioning mind that I admire greatly. Your gifts are certainly beginning to shine."

Traveller helped Whitney to her feet just as Aiden and Ms. Ellie came bursting through the bushes. Whitney winced as she hobbled around testing her ankle. It was obvious the poor girl's ankle was still causing her a great deal of pain, so Traveller suggested, "You can't possibly get all the way back home without help. Aiden and I will walk with you, and you can lean on me for support. I would offer you a ride on my back, but I think the walk will be good for your ankle."

After a slow walk home, they finally arrived at the base of Whitney's stairs. "Before we say good-bye, Whitney, I have one more request. Please don't mention any of this to your mom yet. I want you to know the full story before we involve anyone else. Also, if she's in danger, the less she knows the better. Can you live with that?"

It bothered Whitney to keep secrets from her mom, but she knew it was a wise decision. Keeping her out of danger was more important than keeping secrets. "Okay, at least until I learn more."

Feeling overwhelmed, but excited to see her new friends tomorrow, she waved good-bye and limped up the stairs with Ms. Ellie. Halfway up, she stopped to take a break and turned around. Seeing Traveller standing in the same spot, watching to make sure she made it to the top, Whitney waved once again and shouted, "I hope you find a cozy 'Travellers' Rest,' Traveller!" and grinned. Finally reaching the top, she looked toward the beach once more, but this time there was no sign of the bear or little Aiden and she found herself missing them.

Opening the door to the kitchen, Whitney mumbled, "After what I've heard today, I wouldn't be surprised to learn that our house was named after a talking polar bear named Traveller!"

# Chapter Eight

# MORE SURPRISES

Waking up bright and early, Whitney raced to the kitchen, excited to head back to Ellie's Point. Amazed that her ankle pain was completely gone, she knew she could handle the long walk. After filling her insulated bottle with water and tossing two granola bars, a couple of apples and some kitty treats into her backpack, she headed out the back door with Ms. Ellie close on her heels.

"I'll see you later, mom. I'm going rockhounding."

"Make sure you get home in time for dinner, Whitney. Hey, by the way, I listened to the weather forecast on the radio this morning. We're supposed to get hit with a storm by late afternoon," Susan called from her office.

On her way to the point, Whitney remembered Traveller's promise to answer all of her questions today. She got excited as soon as she saw the bear and ran to meet her.

"Hi Whitney. I'm happy to see that your ankle is no longer causing you problems. I have much to tell you today so let's get comfortable."

Whitney spread her towel on the sand and sat down then looked expectantly at the bear. Smiling at the young girl's enthusiasm Traveller dove into her story. "I'm an Elder on Yagdi, the world where I live. Over many years, I've become a skillful protector. Saving our way of life has become critical because there are evil forces who want to seize control and rule our land. Their threatening actions have become more frequent and need to be stopped. I have devoted my entire life to defending fellow Yagdians. Protectors like me have also sought out and protected others with abilities they aren't aware of. Given the proper training they've been quite helpful allies in saving my world."

Looking carefully at her young friend, Traveller continued quietly, "You are one of those chosen ones and you need my protection, Whitney. Your father was a chosen one too. There are others like you being protected all around your world."

Whitney's eyes widened in disbelief. Staring at the bear, she wrapped her arms around herself protectively with hands fisted as memories of her nightmare flooded back. "Do the evil creatures you speak of ride the mist?" she whispered. "And do they have tentacles on their heads and bright red eyes?"

"Yes, those are our enemies, and they grow stronger by the day. Just a month ago, they found a way to access our personnel files. In doing so, they uncovered the identities of some of our chosen ones. That's how they found out about you. They don't know yet where you live, but can reach you through your dreams, as you've unfortunately discovered. We can talk more about this at a later date, but for now you must know both you and your mother are under my protection, just as your dad was."

Traveller's eyes shone with unshed tears, but she fought them back and continued, "I am so very sorry you lost your father and feel personally responsible. I've lived with my own guilt for almost thirteen years now and still feel as devastated as I did the night of that horrible fire."

Staring at her friend's anguish, Whitney felt her anger lessen, only to be replaced by so much sadness she choked back her own tears. Unsure she wanted to hear the answer to her next question, she asked softly, "Do you think your enemies caused that fire, Traveller?"

Proud of how skillfully the young girl used clues to figure things out, Traveller answered, "Yes, I have always known that to be true, but I could never prove it. The storm was so awful it seemed otherworldly indeed. Following your father's death, I looked for answers to that very question, but I kept running into dead ends. Over time, the clues simply dissolved with no more leads to follow. Yes, I do believe their evil deeds were behind the devastating fire that caused your father's death. That's why I stayed on Earth for several years after your father passed away. I needed to watch over you and your mother until I felt certain you were no longer in danger."

Whitney nodded in understanding then asked, "How much danger are my mother and I in?"

"I gave the moonstone to your father as protection, but he went into the fire without it. Now it's yours for the same reason. As long as it's on you, it will find a way to protect you. Although your mom is an incredible woman and mother, who has wisely recognized her daughter is special, she is not a chosen one. However, she may be in danger simply because she's your mom."

Watching Whitney carefully, the bear continued, "I've returned to protect both you and your mom, for as long as it's necessary. I'll be a very fierce protector, because I am learning to care a great deal about both of you."

Whitney paled and she covered her eyes. As tears fell down her cheeks, she whispered, "How can I be expected to accept all of this? What do you mean when you say I'm 'chosen' to help save your world? Why me? I'm just a kid!"

Traveller answered sympathetically, "I know you're afraid of changes you can't understand. I want to help you figure out what's happening. I also want to assist you in discovering your unique gifts, then learn to use them. I'll be your guide and we'll progress at a pace you're comfortable with. I realize it's a lot to accept. However, I hope you learn to embrace your gifts, dear Whitney."

Whitney's expressive face still reflected devastation and

confusion. Convinced it was time to tell the young girl the entire story about herself and her father, Traveller gently began, "Whitney, the way we identify 'chosen ones' like you, is an intriguing story. Yagdians are always looking for allies, both inside and outside of our world, so we're constantly probing other worlds far from our own. That's how we discovered your Earth. We were pleased to find your world has an abundance of gifted creatures. Our elders have become quite adept at recognizing those with gifts that exceed normal talents. You were identified as a chosen one at birth."

Traveller was growing so fond of this girl and knew this had to be extremely difficult for the girl to hear. However, the bear also knew it was all critically important for Whitney to learn, so she took a deep breath and continued. "There is another protector living with you and your mom. The day you found your 'Ms. Ellie' was the day you brought in a very capable guardian. If you or your mom were ever in danger, she would become a much larger, extremely protective beast. Ferocious by nature, her true form on Yagdi is a majestic black panther. Ms. Ellie and I talked yesterday, before you arrived. She reassured me she felt capable and prepared to protect and defend you and your mom. Your little cat also admitted she's grown quite attached to both of you. I can personally assure you that's a powerful motivator, young Whitney." The bear paused and watched the girl's reaction, ready for a predictably strong response.

Whitney just sat there, dismayed at how overwhelmed she'd become. Moaning, she cried, "What on earth am I supposed to do with all of this?" The bear simply waited, not quite sure how to answer that question. Rising, Whitney put her hands on her hips defiantly and stared at the bear. When she finally spoke, her arms flew through the air, as if punctuating each statement.

"You're telling me that our little cat, Ms. Ellie, is a giant ferocious black panther in disguise! Traveller, this is all way too much for me to believe. I can't make sense out of anything you've told me! You've caused me to question my eyesight, and now my hearing, in just two days!"

Whitney tried to ignore the bear's twitching mouth and felt offended that her 'friend' found humor in her emotional outburst. Putting her hands back on her hips she continued, "This is what you've just told me." Holding up one finger, Whitney shouted, "Bombshell Number One, I've been identified by your elders as a chosen one, just like my father. Let's not forget I never had the chance to meet him or feel his love because he died the night I was born." Putting two fingers in the air, Whitney continued, "Bombshell Number Two, I need protection from the evil mist creatures who want to wrap their tentacles around me and pull me out of my nightmares and into some strange world I know nothing about." Three fingers went up next and Whitney felt herself getting more and more worked up. "Bombshell Number Three, you insist you're here to protect my mom and me and we didn't even know we needed to be protected! By the way, I thought that was what our fierce little kitty was supposed to do! Speaking of our little house cat," Whitney paused to raise four fingers high into the air and finished her rant, "Bombshell Number Four, we have unknowingly been sharing our home with a fierce Yagdian posing as a house cat. Oh, and let's not forget the best one of all. I'm having a conversation with a Yagdian polar bear on the shore of Lake Superior! Have I left anything out?"

The bear's humor had turned serious and thoughtful during her rant. Grateful the bear had actually acknowledged her frustration, Whitney stopped pacing and admitted softly, "Can you see how unbelievable this all sounds? It's so hard to make sense out of everything you've just told me. I'm working hard on the believing part. Please say there's no more, because I'm already in full-blown overload."

When she saw the bear frown and look away sheepishly,

Whitney's voice trailed off and she said softly, "Oh no, there is more, isn't there?"

A long period of silence went by as Traveller carefully considered how much more to share today. Impatiently Whitney prompted her friend, "Okay, Traveller, I need to get home before I grow old enough to vote, and I know there's something else, so please spill it!"

Wisely determining the details could wait until the next day, the bear decided she could at least give the girl a hint of yet one more 'bombshell.' "Yes, there is more, Whitney. But I promise that this next revelation will make you feel less alone. There is another chosen one nearby. Like you, he's been struggling with changes that he can't understand. I'd like the two of you to meet. After that, we can all work together to create a plan that will use each of our unique gifts. An alliance of three could be extremely powerful! Can we just leave it at that until tomorrow?"

Extremely curious about this other chosen one and reluctant to once again say good-bye, Whitney realized she was more than a little bit jealous that there was another like her close by. "Can't you at least give me a hint?"

Grinning, the bear said, "It's someone who just moved to the area. I think you'll get along splendidly, that is after the awkward introductions. Fortunately, or unfortunately, you're very much alike. Time will tell if that's a hindrance or help."

A bolt of lightning, followed closely by a loud thunderous boom, made them both look to the sky. It had grown ominous while they'd been distracted by their conversation. In fact, the wall of clouds seemed to grow thicker and darker by the second. Just then, Whitney remembered her mom's weather warning that morning and sensed it was past time to head home. Agreeing to wait until the next day to discover more about this mysterious chosen one living close by, they said a hasty farewell.

Just then, Aiden and Ms. Ellie raced toward them from their

day of mysterious adventures. They both looked to the sky as they ran and seemed to be more than a little concerned about the approaching storm. Getting down on her knees, Whitney opened her arms for the little dragon to eagerly rush into. Licking her face energetically, he made her feel like she really mattered to him. Giving him quiet reassurances and a hug, she put him down, stroked the colorful scales on his little head and whispered, "You act just like a puppy, little Aiden. Will you promise to take good care of our big furry bear until we meet again?"

Picking up her ferocious little cat, she was turning to leave when she caught the now familiar, "There's one more thing," look on Traveller's face and waited expectantly.

"Speaking of puppies, young Whitney, you see a cute little dragon because of your special gifts. When others look at him, your mom for example, they will simply see a cute little puppy."

Easily navigating this new information, Whitney quickly admitted, "I'm very pleased I can see this cute little dragon. I guess I should say 'lucky me!'" Smiling at each other, they waved and yelled a final farewell over another loud thunderous ka-boom!

Although these past two days had been difficult, Whitney admitted she couldn't wait to hear more of her friend's mind-blowing revelations tomorrow. Headed home, another bolt of lightning raced across the sky, immediately followed by thunder. Putting her cat down, Whitney started to run and yelled, "Come on Ms. Ellie, we'd better hurry home before we get soaked!"

# Chapter Nine

# A VIOLENT THUNDERSTORM

The storm hit hard and fast while Whitney climbed the stairs to her house. Racing the short distance to the back door, Whitney and Ms. Ellie both got soaked! As they walked in, the ceiling lights flickered prompting Whitney to mumble, "We might need to read by candlelight tonight."

Turning to close the door, Whitney saw a huge bolt of lightning cross the sky. It illuminated a large bank of low, dark clouds that extended as far as she could see in every direction. Each of the clouds looked like a mighty dragon, and the lightning bolt appeared to come out of the dragon-shaped cloud directly over her house. Seized by an irrational fear that danger was near, Whitney nervously slammed the door.

Running unsteady hands through her hair, she took a deep, calming breath. The brightly lit kitchen with its cheerful yellow walls and soft pink flower sitting on the windowsill helped calm Whitney's nerves. Finding her voice again, she yelled, "Mom I'm home!"

Ms. Ellie looked nervously in every direction, making Whitney wonder if those strange images were bothering her too. Scooping her trembling cat into her arms for a reassuring hug, she whispered, "I'm glad we made it home before the storm gets worse." Looking into her cat's concerned yellow eyes, she cooed, "I know my fierce protector won't let a big bad storm threaten me. But you can stand down, Ms. Ellie. We're safely home. It's just another summer storm. No bad guys will get us in here."

Ms. Ellie looked unconvinced and wiggled to get down. Once on the floor, she remained alert, and stayed right at Whitney's heels as they went looking for Susan. Finding her mom reading a book and looking warm and cozy near the fireplace, Whitney walked up close and rubbed her wet hands by the fire. Susan put her book down and smiled warmly at her daughter. "It looks like this is the summer for storms. I can't ever remember experiencing so many! Why don't you go put some dry clothes on then join me by the fireplace and tell me all about your day."

"How on earth am I going to explain my day to mom?" she wondered, but simply said, "Good idea, mom," and ran upstairs.

Sitting down at her desk, Whitney rested her chin on a closed fist. She had a difficult decision to make before joining her mom downstairs. They never ever kept secrets from each other, but that was before she'd met a talking polar bear and learned their rescue cat was a black panther in disguise.

Whitney felt terribly torn and didn't know what to do. Should she tell her mom everything, or would the best solution be just telling her the parts that didn't seem so crazy? Knowing she'd just lost control and yelled at Traveller, Whitney wasn't sure she was equipped to ease the fears of a raging mother intent on protecting her only daughter! "Oh man, this is tough!" Whitney moaned to herself, as she quickly changed into dry clothes.

Waiting by the fire with hot cocoa for both of them, Whitney's mom passed a steaming mug to her daughter and proceeded to tell her about her productive day. She saw six patients, two of them were cats and four were dogs. Three of them had serious health issues, but "Fortunately, each human 'parent' left relieved and grateful their 'fur baby's' vet was so amazing," Susan ended with a laugh.

Whitney never missed an opportunity to tell her mom how

proud she was of her accomplishments. This time was no exception. "They're so lucky to have found you, mom! You are amazing!"

Taking a deep breath, Whitney nervously wondered, "Which outrageous part of my day should I begin with? The talking polar bear part, or the part where our little rescue cat can turn into a ferocious sleek black panther? Or how about the part where we may need protection from the evil creatures in my nightmare? Man, I've heard it already and it still sounds unbelievable. How on Earth can I expect mom to believe any of it?"

Her mom's safety was most important and forced Whitney to make the only decision that made sense. Right or wrong, she'd have to live with it, so she began, "I had the most amazing day on the beach, mom. I found an agate with the most beautiful rings so full of color. It was the first thing I found and I threw it into the rock tumbler already or I'd show you. There were some amazing pieces of driftwood all over the beach too. I found one that looks like the neck and head of a swan, with a long beak. Do you want to see them?"

At her mom's nod of encouragement, Whitney hurried to get her beach bag, filled with apprehension. Pretty sure she'd done the right thing, she still felt guilty for her intentional deception. "I wish I knew for certain I just made the right choice, because what's done can't be undone," Whitney thought miserably.

After dinner, Whitney and her mom sat at their puzzle table in front of the fireplace late into the evening. The storm outside was fearsome, sending gusts of wind racing past their windows, moaning threateningly and bending small pine trees in half, as if forcing them to bow to its power. The resilient little trees popped back up as soon as the wind subsided, only to bend again under the force of another powerful gust. Torrential rain hit their windows with a noisy rat-a-tat-tat-tat that seemed to accompany the movement of the dancing trees.

Raging for hours without pausing, the storm produced an abundance of lightning. The bright flashes of light split the ominously dark sky and created plenty of loud thunderous 'Ka-Booms!' Whitney and her mom held their breaths each time the lights flickered, hoping they wouldn't have to light their emergency candles in the sudden darkness.

Sitting near the fireplace with her mom, Whitney felt protected from the wrath of the storm. However, she realized she'd become too tired to put sleep off any longer and was unable to stop yawning. Giving up, she kissed her mom good night and walked slowly up the stairs.

# Chapter Ten

# A THREATENING DEVELOPMENT

Crawling into bed, Whitney still tried her best to stay awake. She tossed and turned for a very long time, fluffing and rearranging her pillow too many times to count. Her cat's grumpy behavior, evil eye and all, warned Whitney she'd better give up and go to sleep.

With grim humor, Whitney wondered what would happen if her little Ms. Ellie turned into a ferocious black panther to protect her. She imagined her sleek black body fearlessly attacking each and every evil creature in her nightmare. They wouldn't stand a chance against such wild fury. Whitney sleepily admitted she liked that outcome, a lot!

Noticing the girl's drooping eyes suddenly open wide to stare at her, Ms. Ellie wondered what the girl was thinking about. Whatever it was, it appeared to involve her. Her young bedmate had been moving around restlessly for an hour now, forcing her to get up many times and reposition her body. Sighing with relief, the cat finally saw Whitney's eyes close.

• • •

With great relief, her nightmare began with a joyful celebration. It was a feast for her senses, enticing her to join the fun. Captivated by the beautiful creatures all around her, Whitney saw elegant and stately creatures with bodies shimmering in an ever-changing

73

rainbow of colors spinning delicately with each movement. Their light airy steps looked like a ballet as they floated gracefully above the ground. Gliding to each other, they would pirouette their greeting, then move to the next acquaintance.

Others were roly-poly and cuddly and made her smile. They were friendly creatures; quick to run up to others with welcoming smiles and big hugs.

There were huge bears with massive bodies and thick white fur that looked like her friend Traveller. Of all of the creatures, they seemed the most human-like in their movements because they walked rather than glided. She was curious what made them stride with such purpose, pausing occasionally to stand upright and gaze intently over the meadow teaming with colorful creatures. Were they looking for something?

Suddenly, a giant winged creature flew down from the mountain peaks high above the clouds. He soared in slow graceful circles that brought him closer and closer. Soon the majestic beast was joined by many like him, circling ever closer as they followed their leader. From a distance, they looked like giant eagles. However, as they came closer, Whitney realized they weren't eagles at all but the mighty dragons that had once come to her rescue.

One of them shot a powerful ball of red fire from its long nose high into the air. That one explosion became many as all of them joined in. It was spectacular and reminded her of fireworks on the 4$^{th}$ of July!

They impressed everyone with their light show. Flying with the wind, the mighty beasts soared from the valley floor to the distant mountain peaks in seconds flat. Everyone cheered and waved while breathlessly watching their athletic movements. The day was filled with smiling faces and loud boisterous fun.

Bewitched by the colors and beauty spread out before her like an artist's pallet, Whitney was enjoying herself immensely, and wished she could fly with the dragons. She hoped the leader would fly close once again. As if hearing her wish, the most gigantic of all the dragons left his army to fly right to her.

Hovering a few feet above her, his mighty wings moved slowly, just enough to stay in the air, and he stared down at her. This close, his vivid yellow eyes were huge, and she was able to see amazing details. Surprisingly, they weren't completely yellow at all, but filled with black dots. There was a thick black line going from top to bottom in the middle of each eye that looked very much like serpents. They actually moved with a life of their own each time the dragon blinked his eyes.

Thrilled to see this incredible creature so close to her, Whitney stared back in wonder. Suddenly, one of his yellow eyes winked at her. Surprised, Whitney smiled back then felt her face redden. This majestic creature's unexpected attention had made her feel suddenly shy.

Tipping one huge wing toward her in farewell, the huge dragon rejoined his army. Soaring into the sky, they returned to their homes in the mountain peaks high above. "Wow, that was amazing. It felt like he was thanking me for something," Whitney thought excitedly.

Suddenly, all of the beautiful creatures froze and looked toward something far away. Although she tried, Whitney couldn't see what was frightening them. Frantic movement erupted all around her, and she watched every single one of them scatter in every direction.

Filled with life and color just moments ago, the meadow was now eerily empty and silent. Suddenly feeling very much alone, Whitney wondered what had caused such a frightened reaction.

Baffled at their panicked exodus, Whitney once again peered into the distance. This time, she could see something far away. Cloaked in a dense fog, she couldn't identify what it was, but it appeared to be moving in her direction.

Suddenly, Whitney's heart sank, and she began to shake uncontrollably. In anguish, she realized it was the horrifying mist from her nightmares. It was gliding slowly across the valley floor, bringing its evil mist creatures with the bright red eyes right toward her! This was what had scared the joyful creatures away, which meant they had a common enemy!

A sense of doom settled into Whitney and made her want to run away, just as the colorful creatures had moments before. Paralyzing fear overcame her when she discovered some invisible force was holding her in place. Then she heard the evil creatures speak to her from inside the mist. Stunned, all she could make out was a mumbled language unfamiliar to her. Although she didn't understand the words, their intent was all too clear.

Their bright red eyes, filled with rage, stared at her, and their clawed hands were fisted and pointed at her threateningly. Tossed out of the mist, they began moving toward her far too quickly.

Until tonight, her nightmares had merely interrupted her sleep, forcing her to dream about this faraway land. The creatures in this land, good or evil, had never interacted with her physically, nor had they expected her to interact with them. The evil creatures seemed satisfied conjuring up new ways to terrify her. She feared them, and their mean spirits, but never felt physically threatened.

This nightmare seemed far more threatening. There was a disturbing new development that made her body shiver. Watching the angry mist creatures draw nearer, she was horrified to see they weren't stopped by the normal dream barrier but continued toward her. They were much too close when suddenly Whitney felt her necklace heat up. Knowing this was meant to be a warning that danger was near, she was desperate to run away, but found she was still held by some wicked force.

Confronted with the horrifying thought she might not survive this attack, her enemies were now so close she could almost touch them. She tried to scream, but no sound came out! In shock, Whitney saw the creatures aim their nasty tentacles toward her and fire. Bursting away from their heads, the tentacles sped toward her, growing longer the closer they got.

When the terrifying appendages reached her, they began to wrap around her ankle. Moving higher and higher, they became uncomfortably tight. Finally, her necklace started screaming at her with a heat so intense she couldn't ignore it. "I know there's a threat!" Whitney screamed in anguish.

In shocked disbelief to actually feel something that she thought only existed in her dreams, a new impossible fear began to emerge. What if she could be pulled out of her world, and into theirs? If that was what they were trying to do, they had more in mind than simply terrorizing her.

Whitney now feared for her life! With sudden horrifying clarity, Whitney realized the evil creatures had already successfully pulled her into their world. She was no longer dreaming. It was terribly real. That's why she could feel those tentacles wrap around her! Hoping someone would hear her, she once again screamed "Help!"

With immense relief, she heard a soft reassuring voice whisper, "I'm here and so are my powerful friends. We won't let anything happen to you. As I told you on the beach, I am your protector. I've been doing this a very long time and I'm very good at what I do."

The soothing voice and reassuring words were magically easing Whitney's fear and crippling paralysis. She began to feel a thread of hope wind its way through her heart.

Suddenly, she heard a loud commanding shriek echo through the canyon. Whitney looked toward the sound and gasped as hundreds of magnificent dragons flew toward her fast and low with grim determination. In a well-executed formation, they flew so close to each other, their wings were almost touching. They carried much-needed hope on their powerful wings because they were headed right toward the evil mist creatures holding her captive.

A thundering sound boomed over the barren landscape and made Whitney look toward the walls of the city. Her heart soared at the sight of an impenetrable wall of gigantic bears racing to join the dragons. There was her friend Traveller leading them with fury blazing in her eyes. Fueled by outrage at the actions of their enemies, they approached with lightning-fast speed.

Such a show of bravery and strength caused Whitney to bring her hands up to cheer for them, and she discovered she was no longer frozen in place. Even better, the mist creatures had become so distracted, their tentacles, although still wrapped around her, had loosened.

Wanting desperately to do something to help these magnificent creatures, Whitney looked down at the nasty fingers holding her captive. Helpless anger was suddenly replaced with fierce determination to get them off!

Bracing herself, Whitney shook one leg vigorously. Shocked when one horrible tentacle dropped away, she repeated the motion with the other leg. It worked and she watched with great satisfaction as all the restraining tentacles fell back onto the distorted heads of the panicked evil creatures. She was thrilled that her movements were no longer confined by those horrid things. Realizing the threat to Whitney was no longer imminent, her stones on the necklace began to cool to their normal comforting warmth.

Freeing herself from those shackles made Whitney feel just a little bit stronger, and a victorious smile appeared. Proud of her small accomplishment, Whitney focused on her ferocious protectors.

Traveller roared encouragement to her bear clan as they ran fearlessly toward the evil creatures. Their horrid, clawed fists raised in defense looked terribly dangerous to Whitney, but certainly didn't deter the bears.

The dragons flew low and directed flaming bolts of red-hot fire with deadly accuracy, right into the middle of the mist creatures. The huge beasts formed a threatening circle in the air just above the mist creatures, then opened just enough to allow their revered leader room to soar past them and right into the heart of their enemy. Hovering menacingly just above the mist creatures, his huge yellow eyes scanned the crowd of deformed monstrosities, pausing to glare at each one in turn. The formidable dragon's huge claws were out-stretched, and he unfolded his razor-sharp talons that were ready to shred any who dared approach him.

The dragon beat his massive wings, sending shards of sand and sharp stones flying into the creatures' faces. Covering their eyes, they cowered in fear before him. Then the King of Yagdi bellowed with unfettered authority, "No more warnings! From this moment forward, our might will be feared by any who dare to threaten my people. That includes our precious chosen ones!"

They were all making her so proud! Whitney felt grateful tears temporarily blur her vision then fall down her cheeks. What had she done to deserve such loyalty, and how could she ever repay them?

Just then, a small group of evil creatures raced stupidly toward the dragon hovering mere feet over them. Their claws were extended and clicking menacingly. In response, flames of fury rained down all around the terrified mist creatures, and instantly incinerated several. Chaos erupted as they tried to get away. As they ran in all directions, they were either met with more bursts of fire or livid bears who were finally able to unleash the anger they'd restrained far too long.

The mist creatures knew they were no match for this ferocious and deadly attack, so they raced with the speed of cowards back into the mist. The bears and dragons roared in frustration when they discovered they were unable to penetrate that barrier.

From their safe enclosure, the monsters raised clawed fists and bellowed, "You are all doomed!" As the mist dragged them away, Whitney clearly heard a loud and threatening promise, "For this land to become ours, the girl, and all of her bears and dragons must be eliminated."

Saddened by such determination in the voices of their enemies, Whitney worried about the mighty protectors of this land. What would happen to all the beautiful creatures if the dragons and bears no longer existed? And what did those mist creatures mean when they called the bears and dragons 'hers?'

Whitney was relieved to see their enemy running away, and so proud of all of those brave creatures. When she saw the majestic dragons turn and fly in her direction, she jumped up and down and waved excitedly while they soared toward her. Passing over her, they flew so low Whitney raised her arms to touch each one who flew close enough to her! However, she was stunned when they tipped their wings as if saluting her. Then the bears circled her, lowered their chests toward the ground and bowed their massive heads.

Whitney suddenly felt self-conscious as unexpected feelings of inadequacy surfaced. Those magnificent creatures had just put themselves in harm's way to come to her defense, but what had she ever done for them? Feeling a sudden unity with the creatures of this land, she bowed low to the bears and saluted the dragons as they flew away.

Traveller stayed behind and walked up to her young chosen warrior with pride in her eyes. Giving her a quick bear hug, she exclaimed, "I am so very proud of you, Whitney!"

The show of loyalty from these amazing creatures had truly humbled her, but Whitney had been able to control her emotions. She didn't think she was worthy of praise from any of them, especially not her friend, Traveller. Now her friend was looking at her with so much pride, Whitney lost the slim control she'd been hanging onto. Throwing her arms around Traveller's thick furry neck, she cried for a long time.

Finally, she stepped back to wipe her eyes, and admitted, "Those magnificent creatures endangered themselves to protect me! They don't even know me. What have I done to deserve such loyalty?"

Feelings of shame and wonder were at war inside of her. "I feel so honored, but I haven't done anything to earn such devotion. My heart aches for your world! As I watched all of you fearlessly attack our enemy, I grew even more determined to help you. I know I'm just a kid, but I'm willing to do whatever it takes to become strong and fearless like you. I want to fight alongside all of these brave warriors to defeat our enemy, once and for all! And yes, I said OUR enemy. Could you help me become that warrior, Traveller?"

Traveller looked in shocked wonder at the resolve on Whitney's expressive face. Thanking the stars for this remarkable turn of events, her face erupted into a huge smile and she looked into Whitney's eyes and promised, "Yes I would be honored to help you become that warrior, young Whitney, and I hope you know how deeply touched and thankful I am!"

· · ·

Whitney woke up just enough to hear soft quiet rain, but no more thunder, lightning or winds. Sighing, she murmured, "Thank Goodness!" then fell into a deep untroubled sleep, unaware her friend remained nearby to guard her as she slept.

At the base of Whitney's long stairway to the beach, Traveller shook the last of the rain off her thick protective fur coat and raised her head toward the stars that began to appear between the few lingering storm clouds. Curling into the comfortable nest she'd dug in the sand, the bear sighed, grateful she felt hope once again. She and Whitney would build a strong alliance indeed. Shaking her head, she remembered everything that had happened, and felt relief when Whitney had finally fallen asleep, safe at least for the rest of this night.

Waking from a short nap, Traveller thought of Whitney. For the first time, the bear's enemies had actually dragged the girl into Yagdi, using her nightmare as a portal. It's just a matter of time before the same thing happened to young Edward. Her enemy's actions were growing more threatening, so she must increase her vigilance. She was admittedly becoming quite attached to these young warriors and murmured, "Keeping them both safe will be so much easier and far more effective when Whitney and Edward meet. Joining forces, we will be a powerful alliance indeed!"

Rising to shake the sand from her fur, the bear's strong legs propelled her toward the point to finalize her plan for today's "chance encounter." Her heart was so full of pride for her brave friends and warriors on Yagdi. She was confident their enemy would soon bring war, rather than continue with these minor skirmishes. However, her army had looked magnificent and fierce. Forcing the retreat of their enemy had saved Whitney from unthinkable consequences.

# Chapter Eleven

## ANOTHER CHOSEN ONE ARRIVES

Morning arrived bright and clear, as if last night's storm never happened. Soothed by the sun's warmth, Whitney opened her eyes and squinted at the bright light streaming through her window. Her pleasant day was suddenly interrupted as horrifying images from last night's nightmare began to return, slithering into her mind just like those terrifying tentacles. Sitting straight up in bed, Whitney's eyes grew wide with fear and she looked nervously around her room. She peered cautiously into every corner and crevasse still hidden in shadows, hoping there wouldn't be any red eyes peeking out at her. Finding nothing but dust bunnies and a lost earring, she began to relax. Falling back onto her pillow, she thought about what had happened last night.

So many things fueled her growing curiosity and bewilderment. It seemed like she'd actually gone to that faraway land and witnessed Traveller and her bear clan join the dragons to battle the evil mist creatures. She had really felt those awful tentacles wrap around her ankles and move up her legs. She'd witnessed a great battle and heard the angry yells. She'd felt her friend's reassuring paw on her shoulder, saw the pride in her eyes and heard her soothing voice. It couldn't have been just a dream. It was too vivid! She definitely needed answers today.

Excited to see Traveller and Aiden again, she knew what her first two questions would be. "Was that really a dream, and did I see you lead a bear clan to my defense?!?"

In spite of her lingering bewilderment from last night, Whitney still thought today should be way less bizarre than all of yesterday's shocking discoveries. She wouldn't have to confront the shock of a talking polar bear on her beach, or the discovery that she was a so-called chosen one under Traveller's protection. She was already adjusting to the fact that her sweet little rescue cat was actually a huge ferocious black panther ready to protect her and mom.

"Yep, the hard part's probably over!" Whitney murmured hopefully. "What could she spring on me that would be nearly as shocking?" Laughing out loud at her own wishful thinking, Whitney knew her friend could very likely have a ton more up her sleeve, each quite possibly more shocking than what she'd already experienced.

Jumping out of bed, she began getting dressed for another day at the beach. Feeling an itch on her right ankle, she bent down to rub it and fell to the floor in anguish. There on her ankle were bruises and what looked like a mark from a giant squid's suction cup. Moaning in distress, she cradled her head and moved it side to side trying to calm down. "There has to be a rational explanation for this new development. I'm adding this to my list of questions for Traveller, and it's going right to the top!"

Not wanting her mom to see her bruises, Whitney put big bulky socks on, then slipped beach sandals over them, instead of her usual flip flops. Finally dressed, she grabbed her beach bag to fill with lunch stuff. Suddenly remembering Traveller's appetite yesterday, she decided to pack more food this time. Tossing the small beach bag aside, she flung her larger day pack over her shoulder and ran downstairs.

Entering the kitchen, she saw her mom on the phone confirming their BBQ with Edward and his grandparents in two days. "Oh great," Whitney thought, "I'm definitely not looking forward to hanging out with Mallory's grumpy brother!" She'd pretend to enjoy it just this once, though, just to make her mom and Edward's grandparents happy.

Her mom hung up while she was grabbing a chocolate doughnut and putting blueberries on her cereal. Pouring herself another cup of coffee, Susan said, "I just talked with Edward's grandma. You do remember they're coming over in two nights, right?" At Whitney's nod, she continued, "Anyway, she was just telling me Edward had a horrible dream last night and left on his bike in very bad mood mumbling something about riding down the beach. Hearing that, I'm more inclined to think Mallory's description of her grumpy brother is accurate. Anyway, I need to run into town for some supplies for our BBQ. Do you need anything?"

Whitney shook her head and said, "I'll be heading to the beach with Ms. Ellie soon. Last night's storm probably washed tons of cool stuff onto the shore, so I'm planning another trip all the way out to Ellie's Point." Pointing to her day pack, she continued, "I'm taking the big bag because I'm feeling pretty optimistic!"

"Now that sounds like my Whitney," Susan said with relief. Remembering what Edward's grandma had said, she laughed and warned, "You'd better be on the lookout for an angry kid on a bike!" Then she grabbed her purse and kissed her daughter, waving good-bye as she rushed out the door.

Feeling guilty each time she intentionally left her mother out of her real plans she stuffed a huge bite of her doughnut into her mouth and mumbled, "How am I going to keep this up without going insane?"

Edward's bad dream had Whitney feeling a bit disconcerted. Was it just a coincidence they'd both had a bad dream on the same night? Shrugging her shoulders, she dismissed it as just that, but looked forward to a nice long chat with Traveller. Her list of questions was growing by the minute! Grabbing her beach stuff, she ran down to the beach with Ms. Ellie.

Traveller gazed out over the lake and watched the rising sun transform lake Superior's dark waters of night into the colorful turquoise blue of a beautiful summer day. "What a 'Superior' view," she murmured, then chuckled at her clever play on words.

Returning to her earlier troubled thoughts, the bear admitted it had been a very long worrisome night. The two young chosen ones must learn how to protect themselves and little Aidan much sooner than she'd planned. Therefore, she was quite pleased at her foresight to bring Whitney and Edward together.

Two weeks ago, she'd conjured up a spell to ensure Edward was selected as a participant by the triathlon Board of Directors. Their perfectly timed event at Iron Mountain in mid-August was just the opportunity she'd been looking for. It brought him close to Whitney for at least part of the summer, and if more time was needed, she would arrange for that too. His grandparents were thrilled to have their grandson living with them, at least most of the time. Now she could watch both of them more easily. It was time for them to meet.

She smiled proudly at the little 'incident' on the beach she'd planned for the two unsuspecting young people. If all went as it should, Whitney and Edward would meet as if by chance. Chuckling at the fireworks that were certain to erupt between them, she headed back down the peninsula to find a nice hiding spot. She couldn't wait to see how her unusual introduction would unfold.

Whitney had her eyes glued to the sand looking for rocks as she slowly walked down the beach. If one caught her eye, she'd stop to examine it. Getting down on her knees in the sand where the rocks hid was a great way to do that. If they weren't worthy, she'd drop them back into the sand and move on. She'd learned a long time ago that lugging a day's worth of rocks could become quite heavy if she wasn't at least slightly picky about what she put in her bag.

Looking up, she spotted a huge pile of rocks way up in the dunes and had to check it out. She hadn't seen it yesterday, so they were no doubt tossed there by the storm's huge waves. Humming a tune, she knelt down in the sand to inspect a particularly beautiful stone.

All of a sudden, a kid on a bike came flying over the peak of the sand dune just a few feet away. Screaming, she covered her head with her hands, tossing the bag and rock into the air.

Edward was enjoying his exhilarating ride more than usual, because it was defusing his fears from last night's horrible dream. He knew he'd been really rude to his poor grandma this morning when he grumbled something about going for a ride, then slammed their door. But those nightmares were wreaking havoc on his sleep, and the one last night was the worst one yet! He'd apologize as soon as he got back.

The special fat tires he'd bought for sand were really getting a workout! For some reason, this morning he'd changed things up and rode a different sandy trail through the woods. It had ended on the beach, where he was excited to discover a row of dunes offering a new challenge. Navigating each one like the pro he was, he felt pushed to his limits, just the way he liked. He'd definitely come this way again.

It wasn't easy to ride a bike through any kind of sand, but it was especially hard going uphill. Downhill was tricky too because your tires could easily bog down in the sand, twisting them enough to throw you off. His leg muscles were screaming, and it felt great! "Take that, nightmares," he thought.

Looking away was his first mistake. Almost to the top of one of the dunes, he became distracted by something huge running across a very long peninsula jutting out over Lake Superior. Committing the #1 biker sin, Edward failed to look where he was going.

At the top of the dune, instead of looking in the direction his

bike was pointed, he was looking away. Hearing a scream, he quickly turned his head and saw he was headed right toward a girl laying in the sand, and it was too late to do anything about it!

Putting on his brakes, Edward's front tire caught in the deep sand and tipped his bike over, tossing him through the air right at her. His last thought was, "Oh man we're going to hit hard!"

Unfortunately, they did hit, way too hard! Whitney saw the biker dude flying at her and tried to roll away. It helped a little because at least they didn't hit head on. She felt his shoulder hit her, then heard him roll away groaning. Her arm hurt, but not terribly. Listening to his groans, Whitney thought he'd probably gotten the worst of their impact. He was laying in the sand a couple feet away, holding his arm and rocking back and forth. Immediately concerned the poor kid was really hurt, she crawled over to him and asked, "Are you OK?"

Upset with this entire day, the night before and for that matter, an entire month of bad nights, Edward was suddenly furious. Sitting up, still holding his arm, he yelled, "Why the heck were you hiding behind that dune? My poor bike. Look at it!" She was shocked. How could he be blaming her for something that was entirely his fault? However, she admitted his bike didn't look too good with the tire all bent out of shape. For a nano-second she felt bad for this kid, but it didn't last.

91

No longer fearing he'd die on her, Whitney jumped up, put her hands on her hips and stared directly at him. He noticed she looked kind of cute all puffed up and angry like that. Shaking his head, he felt like slapping himself and wondered where on earth that had come from! Holding his arm, he stood up watching her the entire time. His eyes shot daggers as his fury rose. How dare she look at him like he'd done something wrong!

They simply stared at each other, neither wanting to look away, until Whitney yelled, "Why are you riding in the sand anyway? That's just stupid!"

Edward yelled back, "Lots of people ride in the sand. It's a great work out, but you wouldn't know about that, would you? No, you just want to hide in it. Who does that, anyway? I've never seen anything remotely like what you were just doing, so why would I be looking for it?"

To that Whitney spit out, "For two years I've been walking this beach, and haven't run across anyone on a bike going full speed and not watch where they were going! If you're such a biker dude, you should know better! Everyone knows that rule, even people like me who 'hide' in the sand!"

"Now that's not fair. You didn't know I wasn't looking!" Edward explained.

"Oh, so now you admit you weren't looking!" Whitney huffed pleased with herself.

That did it, Edward was now so angry he wasn't thinking straight. Seeing her precious bag, he picked it up and turned it upside down, so all her stuff fell into the sand saying, "Take that!"

Whitney was seething. "I can't believe you just dumped all my things!" then punched him in the stomach, immediately stepping back to rotate her hand, making sure nothing was broken. Then she added, "Don't you ever touch anything of mine again!"

Shocked, Edward rubbed his stomach and yelled, "Hey, I didn't deserve that! Do you smack everyone you get upset with?

You pack a mean punch. Serves you right if you hurt your hand! Who taught you how to fight anyway?"

Their yelling lapsed into a silent stare down, with neither wanting to back off and look away. Edward secretly admitted he admired this girl's spirit. At the same time, Whitney was tired of this irritating kid on her beach and murmured to herself, "Where'd he come from anyway?" Out loud, she answered, "I'll have you know you're the first person to receive that honor, and it's well deserved!"

Edward gave in first. Raising his hands in defeat, he grinned sheepishly. Whitney eyed him suspiciously, but quickly decided it looked more like it was his attempt at apologizing, lame as it was, so she grinned back. Continuing to stare at each other, both were beginning to realize how ridiculous this situation was. It had gotten way out of control. Their grins turned into chuckles that immediately broke out into uncontrolled laughter.

Whitney's emotions had been riding high for a month now and releasing them in a good old-fashioned shouting match had felt really good! Wiping her tears away, she noticed Edward was still holding his arm and chuckling as he watched her.

She stuck out her admittedly sore hand saying, "Hi, I'm Whitney and I want you to know that punch was honestly a first for me. I don't usually go around hitting people just because they're irritating. You really bring out the best in a girl, don't you!"

She gasped when he smiled and took her outstretched hand and said, "Thanks for the compliment, I think. It's nice to meet you, Whitney. I'm Edward."

Looking at Edward, Whitney thought, "No way! This couldn't be Mallory's brother!" However, she needed to make sure. "Hey Biker Boy, do you by chance have a sister named Mallory?"

Now it was Edward's turn to look shocked. "You're not my sister's letter-writing friend, are you?" When Whitney nodded, he shook his head in disbelief. "I had you pictured all wrong.

From Mallory's description, I thought you'd look like a librarian with mousy brown hair and big glasses, not a suntanned athlete." Then looking sheepish he said, "Sorry, Whitney."

Whitney grinned and admitted, "I pictured you being small and skinny because it seemed like the best body build for a biker kid. You're neither. In fact, I'm surprised at how strong you look. That can't be important for biking, is it?"

Edward explained, "In fact, you need some serious leg muscles to compete, something I've done for four years now, since I was ten."

Quickly calculating, Whitney figured he was one year older than her. Just then her stomach grumbled. She realized the morning was almost gone, and she had to get out to the point. But first, she needed to retrieve all the stuff he'd dumped in the sand, so she started crawling around quickly picking things up and putting them back in her bag.

Watching her, Edward felt terribly guilty for letting his temper get away from him. It was something he'd done way too much this past month. Getting on his knees, he helped Whitney pick everything up.

Feeling she should at least offer to help him get his mangled bike home, Whitney offered, "I was planning on walking out to the point this morning, but I could help you take your bike back first. You're being careful with your arm. It must be really painful."

He answered, "Na, let's just leave it here. I'll walk with you for a while to give my arm a chance to feel better then limp the poor thing home. I'm curious if we'll see anything out there. I admit I was looking the wrong way because I saw something huge running on the peninsula. That's why we collided."

Knowing exactly what he'd seen, Whitney tried to figure out how NOT to take him with her. Pondering what to do next, she was struck with a genius idea. Considering the pros and cons, she decided, "Maybe he should walk out there with me. Traveller said the new chosen one had just moved to the area. Edward had. The new chosen one was a boy. Edward was a boy. This area isn't crawling with people, so it seems likely Edward is the new chosen one. How interesting. I think I SHOULD take him out there and see how this plays out."

When they finished picking up her stuff, Whitney smiled and helped Edward stand. "I'd love company, Biker Boy, and you'll love the view. It's really a special place." He smiled back and they headed out, walking slowly for Edward's sake. Watching him out of the corner of her eye, Whitney thought, "Mallory was so wrong when she said he was just cranky all the time. I might actually grow to like her biker brother."

Unaware there was a very pleased looking bear following them, they talked and laughed as if they'd known each other for years. However, as they got closer to the point Whitney began to worry that her idea might backfire. "This could be interesting in ways I can't even begin to imagine. I hope this was a good idea! Traveller better see us coming and have a darned good plan."

# Chapter Twelve

# EDWARD AND URSULA MEET

Whitney and Edward discovered they had a lot in common and enjoyed each other's company as they walked to the point. In fact, before they knew it, they were approaching the enormous white pine tree surrounded by a ring of smaller pines on the end of the Peninsula. That reminded Whitney of the first time she'd seen the towering tree when she was just a kid. Pointing to it, she said, "When I was a little kid, I created fantasies about that tree. The smaller circle of pine trees were the guardians of their 'master' standing tall in the middle. When I played under that huge tree, I felt safe and secure, as if protected within a fortress of branches hanging down to shelter and protect me."

Edward smiled picturing a younger Whitney with her creative imagination and said, "That's a white pine, right? Isn't that Michigan's State Tree? They can be over a century old!"

Impressed with Edward's knowledge of their state tree, she added, "Yep. They've actually found some that are 500 years old right here in Michigan! This one's so wide I still can't reach all the way across, from one side to the other, with my arms spread wide, and I bet you can't either!"

She'd just sat under that huge tree with Traveller yesterday, so she scanned the area for any signs of the bear, little Aiden or even her cat for that matter. She didn't see any of them, but she saw someone else sitting under her giant tree and murmured, "Oh no, there's someone else here."

Hearing her dismay, Edward asked, "You sound surprised someone else could be here. Why wouldn't people come here? This is a great spot to hang out on a hot summer day."

Whitney's nerves were jumpy because someone was in their meeting place, so she rudely spit out, "Earth to Edward, where were you when we walked all the way out here? Yes, Edward, of course people come to the beach. But do you really think they'd want to carry all their stuff this far? Geeze!" Pointing to the elderly woman sitting in a beach chair under her huge tree, she said, "To answer your question, yea I'm surprised to see that elderly woman sitting in a chair at the end of the point with her umbrella and picnic basket!" Noticing Whitney's good spirits had vanished, and she seemed on edge, Edward let it go and just shrugged his shoulders.

In the meantime, Whitney was getting more and more confused because there wasn't anyone or anything in the area except that woman. Wondering how this day could get any more messed up, she heard a sweet familiar voice yell, "Yoohoo, young Whitney, come over here and join me."

Whitney was stunned because the voice sounded so much like Ursula's from the jewelry store. However, that seemed quite impossible, given the fact she was so elderly. The jeweler she'd met wouldn't be able to walk all the way to the end of Ellie's Point carrying all this stuff!

Once again, the woman shouted excitedly, "Come on, Whitney. It's so beautiful in here. Join me and bring your friend. A lovely little black tigress has found me already."

Not many cats chose to hang out on the beach, so Whitney was quite certain this stranger was talking about her Ms. Ellie. Edward followed close behind Whitney as she walked through the ring of pine trees then toward the woman with the sweet voice sitting under her huge pine tree. Knowing she was uneasy about something he began to feel uncomfortable himself.

Drawing closer, Whitney confirmed it was Ursula, so she demanded, "How on earth did you get all this stuff out here?" The woman grinned and waved it away like it was inconsequential saying none of her stuff was as heavy as it looked.

There on her lap, purring contentedly, was her Ms. Ellie. Ursula's picnic basket contained a lunch that was big enough for a crowd. It almost seemed like she'd been expecting them. She'd packed grapes, Oreo cookies, chips, apples and, barely showing but there, cat treats.

Whitney thought this was getting more mysterious by the minute and wondered why Ursula would've brought treats for a cat, unless she expected to see a cat. The whole thing felt so crazy.

The sweet woman rushed to Whitney with her arms out and gave her a big hug like they were long-lost friends. "Hello to you too, Whitney. It's so nice to see you once again!" Then, she stuck her hand out to Edward and said warmly, "My name is Ursula, and you must be Edward. It's so nice to finally meet you, young man!"

Now it was Edward's turn to be surprised and he thought, "How on earth does she know who I am?" However, he shook her hand politely and mumbled, "Nice to meet you."

Ignoring his confused expression, Ursula just grinned, sat back down and motioned to the large blanket laying at her feet. "Come join me!"

She had to go look for Traveller, so Whitney politely declined, explaining, "I'm supposed to meet someone out here and should look around for her, but thanks for the invitation. Edward, if you want to stay here and have lunch, by all means, be my guest."

Smiling, Ursula suggested, "I've been out here for over an hour and haven't seen anyone come by, other than the two of you that is. I'm certain we can see your friend arrive from here. You might as well enjoy lunch while you're waiting."

Whitney admitted she was hungry, and the woman's argument

made sense, so she accepted the nice woman's invitation and sat down on Ursula's blanket. Putting her bag next to the picnic basket she offered, "I brought lunch too. In fact, I packed for an army. Can we add it to the pile?" Ursula nodded with a grin, secretly knowing why the girl had packed so much."

Leaning back onto her hands, Whitney talked non-stop nervously. "Ms. Ellie, I wondered where you'd gotten off to. It looks like you found a new friend, with treats tucked away in that picnic basket. No wonder you left me. Come here!"

The cat immediately jumped off Ursula's lap to curl up between Whitney and Edward on the blanket. "May I give her one of your treats, Ursula?" Whitney asked.

"Certainly. That's why I brought them." Ursula answered. Then she chuckled at their confused expressions and said, "Looks like it's time for explanations. Whitney, how's your necklace working out?"

Glad to have a normal question, Whitney answered, "I haven't taken it off yet, because I like having something of my dad's close to my heart." Surprising herself with such a private admission to two strangers, she wondered what had gotten into her.

Ursula was as exuberant as Whitney remembered and clapped her hands to say, "I'm thrilled for you, Whitney, and I think you're so smart to keep it on. Remember those tales I told you. If they hold true, the three stones on your necklace will find a way to keep you safe." Whitney nodded, remembering the exciting tales the jeweler had shared.

"What happened to you?" Whitney asked. "When we returned to pick the necklace up, you weren't there. Poor Randolph told us he didn't know anything about you being in his store!"

Looking carefully at the girl, Ursula answered as truthfully as she could, and only left out a little bit. "That poor man. He's so sweet, isn't he? He's absolutely correct when he said he was unaware I'd been in his shop. I was only there to help you, young Whitney! Once you'd picked out the leather cord for your stones, I had to run and left the completed project with Randolph."

Suspecting a small deception, Whitney began to ask another question, but Ursula quickly turned toward Edward with a question of her own. "And Edward, are you wearing your stone?" Edward's mouth popped open in surprise, too stunned to answer her, so she continued, "That Merlinite has wonderful powers too that I'd love to tell you about if you're interested."

Edward couldn't take his eyes off Ursula. The minute he'd seen her up close, he'd been wracking his brain trying to figure out who she reminded him of. However, for the time being he simply nodded and said, "I haven't taken it off either, see?" Then he pulled it out from under his T-shirt.

Whitney gasped at its beauty. Edward's Merlinite was white and black, but it looked like it had some Lake Superior quartz in it too because it had bands of shimmering crystal. "May I see it up close?" Whitney asked. When he nodded, Whitney moved in to hold his stone in her hand. Up close, she saw indigo along with the black and white, and sure enough that was quartz shining in the sunlight. It was magnificent.

Dropping it, she looked at Edward and said, "Sorry, but I'm a rock freak. I'm always looking for beauties like yours, which is what I was doing when you flew into me." She said smiling, "I'll show you my necklace," and pulled it out.

While Edward was looking at her three stones, she thought curiously, "Other than mom and Ursula, no one has seen this necklace. What prompted me to show it to Biker Boy?"

When Edward let go of her necklace, she moved back to her spot on the blanket. He surprised her by admitting, "I love your stones. They feel so warm, though. Is that normal?" Whitney looked terribly confused and appeared to be momentarily speechless, so Edward decided it was best to drop that subject for the time being. However, he asked, "Is that a moonstone in the middle?"

Shocked that he'd felt the heat from her stones and could identify her moonstone, she heard him admit, "I have a curiosity about rocks too. I pick them up occasionally on my bike rides. I have a bunch in a jar at home."

Baffled by Mallory's brother, Whitney just shook her head and stuffed a big juicy grape into her mouth.

Noticing how they had both tucked their stones back inside their shirts, Ursula smiled and broke in, "You both have amazing stones. Edward, you probably don't know Whitney's special moonstone is a gift from her father."

Edward looked expectantly, wanting to hear her story, but Whitney just shrugged her shoulders and said, "That's a story for another time."

Ursula continued cheerily, "You've already heard the tales about your unique stones, Whitney. Would you both like to hear about Edward's Merlinite?"

Excited to hear more of Ursula's amazing stories, Whitney nodded eagerly, so Edward agreed saying, "I'm in!"

Clapping her hands in excitement, she began. "First and foremost, as you may have already deduced, Merlinite is named after the Wizard Merlin, from the legends of King Arthur you have no doubt read." They both nodded so she continued, "It's also known as 'Mystic Merlinite,' and comes from Madagascar. Stories shared through generations, as in Whitney's stones, say if you wear Merlinite close to your heart, it will help you discover special gifts you may not be aware of. It's meant to assist people with extraordinary gifts like invisibility, seeing into the future, and even strong intuition which is more a whispered feeling than fact-based knowledge. That's quite an elusive concept but intriguing enough to learn more."

Noticing their skeptical expressions, Ursula continued, "Mystic Merlinite is the perfect stone to wear if you're still unaware of your own unique talents. One of Merlinite's best features is its ability to calm any troubling concerns. The stone can strengthen your intuition, which helps you identify and understand the cause of your dark thoughts. In other words, for those who sense they may be different, but don't understand it, the stone can help guide your path toward understanding," and looked toward Whitney.

Sitting back to let her words soak in, Ursula took a big gulp from her flask of water and watched each of her chosen ones carefully. When they finally looked at each other and shrugged their shoulders, she continued slowly, weighing her words carefully.

"You are both chosen ones I have come to protect. Your stones were given to each of you because they enhance your unique gifts still buried quite far beneath the surface." Their stunned quizzical expressions begged for more information which she was eager to provide.

"Young Whitney has met me both in the jewelry store and on the beach." As she said this, her body morphed from Ursula to a giant polar bear then back to Ursula once again. It all happened so quickly Whitney gaped then rubbed her eyes to check the accuracy of her vision. Ursula had apparently made sure Edward hadn't seen her transformation, because he just sat there quietly waiting for her to continue.

Seeing Edward's calm demeanor, Whitney frowned and decided to call her friend out. After last night's events, she'd had enough and couldn't wait any longer for answers.

# Chapter Thirteen

## TIME FOR ANSWERS!

She was a nervous wreck. She'd been thrown off when they'd walked up on Ursula sitting under her tree. Then when she saw Ursula transform into Traveller just now, it was the last straw. There were too many secrets, and that was never very healthy. Leaping off the blanket she began to pace. Noticing Edward's shocked expression and Ursula's calm demeanor, she walked purposely up to her and got down on her knees to look into her eyes.

Ursula's big brown eyes showed surprise at this turn of events. Whitney frowned at her friend and demanded, "Ursula, if you're actually my friend Traveller, I have questions for you that can't wait!"

Noticing her friend's hesitation to reveal her true identity to Edward so quickly, Whitney continued, "Edward's a big boy. I think he can handle it. In fact, I think we owe it to him. Don't you think it's time we moved forward?"

Ursula was shocked at Whitney's unexpectedly forceful demand, but also quite impressed. Maybe last night's unplanned trip to Yagdi sparked something buried deep inside of the young girl. She smiled approvingly at Whitney's sudden bold action. Nodding her head, she winked at the girl and transformed into her true form.

"Whoa, come on! What's going on here?" Edward's mind was jumping all over the place trying to figure out what had just happened. Jumping up to run away, he got tripped up by the blanket and fell forward. Landing hard, he got a mouthful of sand. "That didn't help!" He moaned and turned over hugging his arm while spitting out sand.

Whitney started to laugh, but hearing his moan, stopped abruptly. Running over to help him up, she looked at the arm he was holding and asked, "Are you okay?"

Embarrassed he'd fallen in front of Whitney and Ursula, or whoever she was, Edward quickly assessed he just had a sore arm and bruised ego. Angrily jerking his arm away from Whitney, he stood there glaring at both of them. "Can someone tell me what's going on here?" he demanded.

Whitney and the bear looked at each other but it was Traveller who jumped in first. "I know this is a shock, young man, but Ursula and I are one and the same. My name is Traveller and I'm from a world known as Yagdi. I transform into human form while I'm on earth because I'm quite certain a polar bear strolling down Main Street, USA would create a bit of a panic. Wouldn't you agree? Therefore, I thought turning into a very sweet older lady no one in their right mind would fear made perfect sense."

Edward simply stared at the polar bear talking so casually about changing forms, while admitting she wasn't even from earth. Finally, he admitted, "This is too bizarre. I don't even know where to begin to try to understand!"

Whitney jumped in to explain, "Edward, I'm sorry I started to laugh. I really wasn't laughing at you. I actually understand how you feel because I had the same exact reaction to Traveller yesterday. I fell forward and got a mouthful of sand too, but I actually twisted my ankle when I fell."

Edward collapsed back onto the sand and looked pitifully confused, so Traveller turned back into her human form and announced, "How about we have lunch and save our serious discussions for after."

Smelling the sandwiches, Aiden ran out of his hiding place and jumped into Whitney's lap, excited to see her. Once again, she was caught off guard by his enthusiastic greeting and fell backward with the little dragon energetically licking her face. Laughing, she said, "It's good to see you again too, little Aiden." Then she caught sight of Edward's shocked expression.

If Whitney had any lingering doubts that Edward was another chosen one, they vanished when she saw his reaction to the little dragon giving her kisses. He definitely saw Aiden was not a cute little puppy. The look on his face was so priceless she laughed out loud.

"You've got to be kidding me!" Edward shouted, kicking up sand as he frantically scooted backward in an effort to put distance between himself and this strange new creature. He kept his eyes on the little apparition before him while he got up to pace back and forth. Every once in a while, he'd shake his head and run his hand through his already messy hair, making it even more disheveled. Whitney giggled thinking, "That's probably what his brain looks like right now as he tries to figure this out!"

As if hearing her, he stopped and looked first at Ursula then Whitney and shouted in irritation, "I don't know what's going on here, but it's not funny!" It was obvious they were both trying hard not to laugh, so he glared at them, then peered skeptically at Aiden.

The only one not included in his wrath at the moment was Ms. Ellie who was sitting there calmly grooming her face.

Not quite finished yelling, he pointed at them accusingly, "I feel like you all know the punchline, and I haven't even heard the joke!"

Taking pity on him, Whitney put the little dragon down and stood up to coax softly, "Sit down, Biker Boy. I admit I have an advantage right now because I've already gone through the shocking introduction stage. Once you calm down enough to listen, though, you'll soon know as much as I do."

Looking at her like she'd grown two heads, Edward threw up his arms in defeat and mumbled, "All I wanted to do was ride my bike today. Now look at the mess I'm in!" Unfortunately, his pitiful outburst was too much for Whitney and Ursula. Unable to control themselves a minute longer, they burst out laughing. Ursula's laugh was high and shrill, sounding almost like bells, while Whitney's was an untamed full out laugh.

Assuming they were laughing at him, he glared daggers. All that did was make them laugh harder, so he sat down once again to put his head in his hands and moaned, "What am I going to do, what am I going to do," over and over again.

Seeing another sad human, Little Aiden reacted just as he had with Whitney. He leaped right into the middle of Edward's lap and began to fill his face with baby dragon kisses from a very large tongue. Shocked beyond belief, Edward shoved the little dragon off his lap and stood up too quickly. Off balance, he once again fell backwards into the sand only to find the little guy back on top of him staring at him with his big yellow eyes and huge happy grin.

He was so cute, and his smile so happy, Edward could no longer resist and smiled back weakly. Stroking his colorfully scaled head, he murmured quietly, "So you think you're pretty cute, huh?" Aiden was so excited to hear him talk in a happier voice, he began to wiggle from the tip of his tail to the end of his long nose, then resumed bathing his face with kisses.

Watching Edward and Aiden, Ursula and Whitey both smiled, but for very different reasons. The elderly woman was pleased another critical connection had be made successfully, but Whitney just thought the two of them looked cute together!

Edward noticed both sets of eyes on him and blushed, admitting, "He is pretty friendly, isn't he!" Jealous at all the attention the little dragon was receiving, Whitney's cat jumped up and began to run circles around Edward, enticing Aiden to leave Edward's lap and chase her. Sitting in the middle of this chaos, all he could do was cover his eyes and shake his head.

Introductions were over for the time being, so Ursula suggested they eat lunch, then settle in for a serious conversation. Thinking that sounded ominous, Edward decided he needed the energy to tackle what lay ahead, so eagerly grabbed a tuna sandwich, then finished it off with everything else offered.

Finished with their lunch, Edward and Whitney leaned back on their hands and watched Ursula eat her apple, slowly and delicately. The morning had produced some crazy revelations. Growing increasingly impatient to continue their discussion, Edward began tapping the drum solo in "Wipe Out" on his knees. Recognizing the beat, Whitney started to hum the guitar accompaniment, prompting Edward to drum even louder. Finished with her apple, Ursula grinned at their little 'battle of the bands.'

Giddy with relief that they'd all met, and everything was going so smoothly, Ursula jumped up and started moving around in her attempt at dancing. Ms. Ellie and Aiden got into the spirit and started to leap and twirl with her. Their antics cracked Edward and Whitney up so much they started laughing, and Ursula soon joined them.

Sitting back down, she took a deep breath and another sip of water. "Tell me about your nightmares, Edward." Whitney realized he had the distinct advantage of already seeing a woman transform into a bear, then back into a woman again and meeting little Aiden. However, she was still impressed at how well Biker Boy had accepted this unexpected question.

He nodded at Ursula, took a sip of his own water, then dove in to explain his nightmares. He said they'd started about a month ago, just after a strange encounter with a woman while riding a biking trail deep in the forest.

Staring at Ursula once again, he said suspiciously, "I knew you looked familiar. That was you, wasn't it, Ursula?" She just smiled and nodded, so he continued. "Anyway, you came out of nowhere and walked onto the trail right in front of me. I had to slam on the breaks to avoid plowing right into you." Looking at Whitney, he added, "Unlike some people I know, she wasn't hiding on her hands and knees." That got the desired glare he'd hoped for.

"I got off the bike, thinking you might need some help because you were so deep in the woods, and very much alone. But when I asked, you just said, 'No, I don't need help, young chosen one. I'm here to help you.' Then you asked me to hold out my hand. Shocked at this whole strange encounter, I held out my hand and you placed this Mystic Merlinite into it. It was attached to the jute cord I'm wearing now. You told me to keep it on all the time because its powers would keep me safe from harm. Then you grinned at me and said, 'no charge' and almost seemed to vanish, you were out of sight so quickly."

Staring at Edward, Whitney was reminded of the story about how her father had gotten his 'lucky moonstone' and said, "It sure sounds like you were the woman in dad's story too."

Ursula answered eagerly, "Your assumptions are both correct. Edward, that was indeed me in the woods, just as I was the woman who gave your father his moonstone, Whitney. And Whitney, you already know I created that necklace for you in the jewelry store."

Beginning to put pieces together that had been puzzling her, Whitney interrupted, "Ursula, you were in my nightmare last night as Traveller. You and your bear clan joined the powerful dragons in a ferocious battle. I think I was actually there!"

Kicking her sandals off, then removing her socks, Whitney's deep bruises and mark from a huge suction cup on her right ankle were revealed.

Ursula gasped and ran to the girl. Kneeling down she began

a careful inspection of the horrid marks that remained on Whitney's ankle.

Edward gawked, wondering how her ankle had become so bruised, and what on earth had caused those big round circles?

Gently rubbing Whitney's ankle, Ursula sat up straight and announced, "Whitney you did indeed get pulled into my world last night. I hated the fact that those nightmares were terrifying you, but I had no idea our enemy had become so powerful they could actually pull you in! Everything you saw last night was very real indeed!"

Turning from Whitney to look directly at Edward, she continued, "Edward, your dreams have been similar to Whitney's. I don't know when, but Whitney's experience last night could very easily happen to you as well."

Ignoring their stares, she took a deep breath and continued, "I've told Whitney much of what I'm about to tell you, Edward, but you must hear it. I expect you will react quite strongly, with understandable shock and confusion. I promise you, however, as strange as it will sound, it's all the absolute truth."

As Ursula began to tell Edward what she'd just heard the day before, Whitney listened and watched quietly, curious how Edward would react. She admired how easily he seemed to accept the bizarre revelations and was able to calm down pretty quickly. "Whether he believes it or not is yet to be determined however," Whitney mumbled to herself.

Whitney lay back on the blanket and folded a beach towel under her head for a pillow. That was an invitation for her cat and little Aiden to move in. They quickly curled up on either side of her and fell sound asleep. Smiling to herself, she relaxed and felt drowsy hearing Ms. Ellie's purrs and Aiden's soft snores.

She must have dozed because all of a sudden, she felt Edward's hands pushing on her shoulders. Rubbing her eyes, she sat up quickly and noticed the sun was low in the sky. "How long have I been asleep?" she asked. Ursula chimed in, "For hours, dear girl, however it allowed Edward and I to have a nice long chat, didn't it, young man."

Edward grinned weakly and said, "Yes ma'am it sure did, but I'm not sure what to make of everything you've told me."

Whitney nodded her head and admitted, "I had the same reaction, but it's growing on me. Did she tell you about being our protector yet?" When Edward nodded, she continued, "How about the doozie about her world being in trouble and we've been 'chosen' to help save it and protect little Aiden here?"

That's when Edward frowned and admitted, "Yea, but that's a tough one to believe. We're just kids, so how can we help save a world?"

Whitney laughed and said, "That was my reaction too, especially after last night." As she said that, she looked meaningfully at Ursula then asked, "How are we expected to help your world, Ursula?"

Ursula looked cautiously in every direction, then answered, "That's exactly where I was headed next. We must move quicker than I'd planned, so I'd like to show you both something very special. It's crucial that no one else discovers what I will soon reveal, so you must both promise to keep it a secret."

Ursula had become deadly serious. After her frequent laughter and good humor all morning, this was a sudden and unexpected change. Sensing something extremely important was about to happen, the suspense was killing Whitney and Edward, but they patiently nodded their solemn promise. This new hint of danger intrigued them, so Whitney mumbled to Edward, "What do you think she's up to?" Shrugging his shoulders, Edward whispered in her ear, "It has to be huge and I can't wait to see what it is!"

# Chapter Fourteen

# A SECRET IS REVEALED

Satisfied with their promises, and noticing their barely controlled restless energy, Ursula stood and walked to the monstrous trunk of the giant white pine tree and immediately transformed into her Yagdian form. Blocking their view, the magnificent bear held out a paw, and touched the letter "C" discretely carved into the trunk and quietly whispered two simple words, "Travellers Rest."

Both kids gasped when an opening appeared in the enormous tree trunk. As if struck by a powerful bolt of lightning, the fissure was surrounded by an orange glow and moved from the ground to the first broad branches above them then began to widen. As it opened, it revealed glimpses of a world beyond the opening and was soon wide enough to walk through. Speechless at the sight, they weren't given time to figure out what had just happened. Ursula was excited to enter and held out her paw to welcome them to her world. Somewhat cautiously, they walked through the opening in the tree trunk and into another world that seemed far different yet somehow familiar.

Pausing to glance back, Whitney's eyes widened to see the opening was gone! They were surrounded by the sights and sounds of Yagdi. She saw huge trees with strange colorful birds singing sweetly as they flew in and out of their monstrous nests. Waterfalls tumbled from towering mountains whose peaks were cloaked in white puffy clouds. The pools of water below them churned with the constant flow of water and held huge orange fish that looked like giant goldfish. They moved leisurely through the water, occasionally swimming close to the surface looking for a meal. Near the surface, the scales on the huge fish burst into a rainbow of colors as the bright sunlight hit them. Looking up, she saw two suns shining in the sky. "No wonder it seems so bright!" Whitney marveled. Glancing over at Edward, she grinned to see he was just as captivated because his mouth and eyes were both wide open.

Traveller laughed and said, "Welcome to Yagdi, young ones!" as she led them down a path that appeared to lead to some high towers that shined brightly in the sunlight. They seemed far away and appeared to be part of some kind of settlement. The path meandered through a beautiful valley filled with enormous wildflowers, and tall grasses. Mist flowed through the other end of the valley. Feeling suddenly uncomfortable, Whitney thought it seemed out of place on such a bright sunny day.

"Hold It!" Whitney shouted as she came to a halt. Edward and Traveller both stopped in their tracks and turned toward her. Assuming Edward had experienced the same images in his dreams, she pointed to the mist and said, "Can't you picture that mist rolling toward us with those horrid creatures riding inside it?" Then she looked toward the mountain peaks and said excitedly, "The mighty dragons live up there, don't they!"

Looking around him, Edward had to agree it looked very much like the land of his nightmares, and his excitement became tempered with a tinge of fear.

Traveller clucked her tongue and said comfortingly, "Whitney you're absolutely correct, but don't worry, dears. Our enemies are quite occupied at the moment defending themselves in another part of our world, thanks to our well-planned offensive. However, we must keep moving because you're both invited to a party."

"Come quickly," she encouraged, "There are a few wonderful

creatures who are excited to meet you both." Picking up their pace, they arrived at the base of the towers in no time. They seemed to be guarding the settlement and were now so high, Whitney had to bend way back to see the top. It reminded her of a castle's fortress, drawbridge and all. The peaks of each tower were decorated with brilliant colorful mosaics and streamers flew proudly in the light breeze.

Hearing music and joyful singing coming from somewhere ahead of them, Whitney ran across the drawbridge toward the enticing sounds. Edward and Traveller followed right behind. Traveller grinned at both of them, thrilled at their excitement.

Rounding a corner right in the middle of town, a huge meadow was spread out before them. The same stream they'd seen in the valley flowed more gently here. Passing through the meadow, it flowed over small rocks and made a soothing waterfall sound.

The scene before them was a feast for their eyes. The meadow was filled with creatures of all shapes and sizes. As they moved, their bodies shimmered with rainbow colors, just like the scales on the goldfish they'd seen. Whitney was excited to recognize all the beautiful creatures she'd seen in her dreams!

Then Whitney saw Traveller's bear clan. Their massive bodies were covered with sparkling white fur and they walked with authority and moved through the crowds in quiet dignity. Their emotions were restrained, and they held their heads high while greeting the other creatures. However, everything changed when they spotted Traveller. Their faces transformed into huge smiles with sparkling eyes as they ran up to circle her and the two humans. With enthusiastic greetings and warm welcomes, they were smothered in bear hugs and eagerly hugged them back, thrilled to be welcomed into Traveller's clan.

Everyone seemed to be in a joyous mood and looking forward to a grand celebration and Whitney hoped the glorious dragons would join the celebration. As if on cue, she saw their disciplined formation circling on the wind as they plunged from their homes in the mountain peaks high above.

Whitney whispered to Traveller, "These are all the amazing creatures from my dreams, aren't they!" Traveller smiled at the young girl's delight, but took the opportunity to remind her, "Yes, but they're not just dreams anymore, are they?"

Whitney nodded and realized in that moment just how dramatically and quickly her life was changing. Smiling, Edward squeezed her hand to pull her into the throng of creatures. Thrilled to be on Yagdi with so many amazing creatures, Whitney laughed and ran forward. Edward and Traveller were equally excited as they ran alongside her.

When the three reached the middle of the celebration, the music suddenly stopped. Silently, all the creatures moved out to circle Traveller and her two chosen ones. Traveller's bear clan walked up to them and lined up. The mighty dragons flew swiftly toward them and swooped down to hover overhead.

Just then, Whitney saw a man approach a megaphone placed on the stage near the musicians. Traveller whispered that he was their 'communicator.' Picking up the megaphone, he tapped it to ensure it was working, forcing some of the creatures to laugh and hold their ears.

Speaking loudly and excitedly, he announced, "Welcome to our Celebration, Whitney and Edward. You are our heroes, and we thank you from the depths of our hearts for what you plan to do for our beautiful world." Whitney gasped and frowned thinking, "I don't have a plan!"

When the enthusiastic clapping had calmed down, he pointed to the mighty leader of the dragons and said with awe in his voice, "You are going to protect our next mighty ruler, Little Aiden, son of Torryn and Aara, from the evil clutches of our enemy!"

Again, he waited for the excited creatures of Yagdi to settle down. Proceeding once again, he pronounced, "Your bravery will be talked about for centuries to come because your willingness to protect one so precious and important to our world will never be forgotten! Let's all salute our young warriors!"

Amidst the wild cheering all around them, Whitney looked up at Aiden's father hovering over her. Torryn looked down at her and winked once again. Knowing his name, and that he was Aiden's father, his wink now carried a whole new meaning.

She was once again embarrassed at what she considered unearned attention and praise and was suddenly filled with dread. What if she couldn't protect this mighty leader's son?

Torryn flew lower, then did something only reserved for rare circumstances. He dropped to the ground to stand right in front of the two young warriors then looked at Whitney, then Edward, then back at Whitney. His eyes reflected his understanding of her feelings of inadequacy, so he bowed low then whispered in a deep voice, "You will protect my son with your hearts and souls. Of that I am certain. He will be safest with you, young Whitney and Edward, I have confidence in your warrior spirits."

Looking toward the beautiful shimmering dragon hovering nearby, he introduced her with great affection resonating in his voice, "This is Aiden's mother, Araa. We both feel honored to be in your presence and want to thank you personally!"

Araa flew down and landed next to Torryn. Bowing low, she spoke in a soft sweet voice, "My son is in very capable hands. Traveller is a mighty ally and will train you well. Please stay safe until we meet again, young chosen ones. Hug my little Aiden close and tell him often how much his parents miss him. Reassure him we will meet again very soon." Whitney saw tears fill her huge yellow eyes, then fall to the ground.

Whitney felt a new resolve building inside her. Knowing how difficult this would be for her own mother helped her understand the depth of concern Aiden's parents must have to send their young son away to keep him safe. With growing respect for

Aiden's parents, and all of these brave creatures, she bowed low to Torryn, then Araa. They nodded their heads and smiled at her then flew back into formation. Whitney was certain they'd just read her thoughts and were relieved that she'd grasped the depth of their emotions. She realized just then they would stop at nothing to keep their son safe from harm.

With the departure of the bears and dragons, Whitney and Edward were now standing alone in the middle of all these beautiful creatures. Suddenly self-conscious, Whitney felt her face heat up. Sensing her embarrassment, Traveller stepped out of the line of bears and ran to them. Rising up, she became so tall she had to bend over to gather them into her arms then whispered softly, "This celebration to honor both of you is wonderful proof you are indeed mighty warriors and protectors of our most treasured young dragon. You will soon prove this absolute truth to yourselves."

Dropping back onto all four paws, she stood between her two young chosen ones and turned toward the crowd of excited onlookers and smiled proudly. The meadow erupted into wild cheering and creatures began to leap up and down clapping excitedly. The line of bears saluted and bowed low while the dragons stretched their huge wings to their full impressive width and tipped them toward the two humans as they flew by. Close enough to touch their iridescent scales, neither Whitney nor Edward could resist that opportunity, so they reached up high as each mighty dragon flew past them.

When she saw Torryn fly toward them, Whitney reached up to touch the leader, and father of little Aiden. When her fingertips touched his scales, she felt her body tingle and remembered she'd had the same reaction the first time she touched little Aiden. All she could do was stare in amazement. None of the other dragons had that effect on her. He was so huge but seemed so gentle and kind and very special indeed.

Winking at her one last time, Torryn rose into the air and led his army back to their homes high in the peaks of the mountains. Wild cheers continued and the music returned along with the singing and dancing. Whitney and Edward became terribly embarrassed as each beautiful creature approached them with greetings and low bows of gratitude.

When the attention was finally off of them and the celebration had returned in earnest, Whitney turned to Traveller and exclaimed excitedly, "I can't believe this whole celebration was about us!"

Beaming at both of them, Traveller answered, "Now everyone knows of your willingness to help us. They also know you'll do whatever it takes to end the troubling threats from our enemy."

Whitney and Edward looked at each other wide-eyed and mouths open. Edward found his voice and croaked, "I don't remember signing up, but I won't let them down. I don't feel worthy though."

In complete sincerity, Traveller said reassuringly, "You are both indeed worthy. I'll help you train until you feel capable and confident in your roles as protectors for our little dragon!" Wistfully looking at of all her friends, she turned away and said, "As wonderful as this celebration is, I fear it's time we head back to your home."

# Chapter Fifteen

# AN AMBUSH

Waving a final good-bye to everyone, the three headed back toward the portal through which they'd arrived. Nearing the end of their journey, they were preparing to leave the beautiful valley when Whitney saw a dreadful and all-too-familiar sight headed their way. Looking over at Traveller, she knew the bear had seen the same thing. Without a word, they all began to run.

Looking back, Whitney was frightened to see the mist gaining on them and began to think they might not make it in time. "What happens if they catch us?" she asked.

The mist was much faster than the three of them, so Traveller stopped and said urgently, "I'll catch up to you. Don't look back, just run as if your life depended on it, because it does!"

Obeying Traveller, Whitney and Edward ran toward the portal as fast as they could go. However, when they heard the bear's loud urgent battle cry, they stopped and spun around.

Their friend was bravely racing toward the mist all by herself. It had stopped long enough to spew out its cargo of nasty mist creatures then rolled back out of harm's way. Their red eyes glowed and yawning mouths screamed with fury as they lumbered awkwardly toward Traveller. Clawed fists were raised menacingly and the tentacles on their heads moved about wildly, then coiled as they prepared to strike.

Shivering, Whitney was all too familiar with those atrocities! Edward stood next to Whitney and saw her shudder. Trying to offer comfort, he grabbed her shoulder. They looked at each other for a moment, wondering what to do next.

Nodding in silent agreement, they ran toward their friend and their enemies. Not knowing what they could possibly do to help, they just knew they had to try. They couldn't let their friend battle these creatures alone!

Traveller had stopped to wait for the onslaught. That allowed Whitney and Edward to catch up to her. They stood proud and tall next to the bear as their enemy approached. Traveller nodded her thanks to each of them, unbridled anger glowing in her eyes.

Turning as one toward their enemies, the bear once again stood on her hind feet with grim determination and released a bolt of lightning from a huge paw. It landed squarely in the middle of the small army, immediately incinerating a few. Undeterred, the rest shoved the fallen comrades out of their way in maniacal determination to get to their enemies.

Something deep inside Whitney seemed to awaken. Unsure where her next move came from, Whitney placed her hands in front of her shoulders, then pushed her arms forward in a strong outward motion toward the approaching hoard of evil creatures.

The front line seemed to wobble as if struck by sudden and ferocious winds. However, it was barely enough to slow them down. Recovering quickly, the mist creatures advanced toward them once again. Whitney repeated her motion again and again. Each time she would successfully slow them down but could never stop them. Recovering quickly, they kept moving toward them with increasing determination.

As their enemy advanced closer, Edward felt an urge to do something, anything, to help. Out of nowhere, he was struck with a crazy idea. Holding his hands high above his head, he swept them away from each other and down toward the ground, creating a huge sweeping arc. Whatever he'd done, several of the creatures in the lead seemed to run into some kind of invisible barrier.

Unfortunately, the barrier didn't last very long, and allowed the monsters to continue toward them once again. Following Whitney's stubborn lead, Edward repeated his movements again and again, only to see their enemies crash into his invisible barrier. Each time they quickly discovered they weren't stopped for long and continued forward, getting ever closer.

Suddenly the sky above them was filled with mighty dragons. They swooped low over the small group of enemies and formed a straight line with their wingtips touching. Exhaling at the same time, they sent a long line of blazing hot balls of fire right into the heart of the enemy.

Dismayed and disappointed at the unexpectedly strong resistance, the creatures turned and ran quickly into the mist which retreated to the other end of the valley.

Traveller seized on the opportunity to get away. Waving their gratitude to the dragons, Traveller told Whitney and Edward to jump on her back. Urging them to grab her thick fur and hang on tight, she carried them quickly through the portal and back to earth safely.

Slipping off Traveller's back they watched as she easily transformed back into Ursula. Edward shook his head and said, "A little heads up before doing something unexpected like shape shifting would help, Ursula."

Beaming at her two warriors, she gushed, "You have such warrior spirits. Now all we have to do is fine-tune those skills that are beginning to surface. Thank you for racing back to help me."

Whitney smiled back and cheered, "You and every single one of those dragons are my heroes, but I'm so glad to be home!"

Noticing the sun appeared to be very close to where it had been when they left Earth, Whitney and Edward looked at each other mystified. Turning to Ursula, Whitney asked, "Is the passing of time different when we go through your portal?"

Ursula said, "Yes, indeed it is. Time passes much more quickly on Yagdi than it does on Earth. Quite handy if you ask me!" Grinning at their shocked expressions she continued, "I think that's enough for one day, don't you? Can we meet again tomorrow?"

Frowning in disappointment, Whitney said, "We have a BBQ tomorrow night. Mom invited Edward and his grandparents over so we could all meet each other. Seems kind of silly now, doesn't it? Anyway, tomorrow might not work."

Whitney would miss seeing Ursula tomorrow, especially after so much excitement today. Struck with a brilliant idea, she asked, "Why don't you join us? Mom would love to see you again, Ursula. But please come as Ursula, not Traveller, Okay?"

Winking at Whitney, she smiled and said, "Ursula graciously accepts your invitation. May I bring Aiden and a dish to pass?" Noticing Edward's frown of concern, she added, "Edward, I forgot to mention that only those with special gifts, like you and Whitney, can see that little Aiden is a dragon. Everyone else simply sees a cute little puppy."

Worried that his grandparents might have been blown away to see a dragon, Edward was relieved and said, "It sounds good to me. What about your mom, Whitney? Will she mind that you invited Ursula without asking her first?"

Answering with complete certainty, Whitney said, "My mom is amazing. She just wants me to be happy and trusts my judgement with people. She'll be glad that we invited Ursula, and her 'cute little puppy' to dinner. My mom's a vet so she welcomes animals of all sizes and shapes, so she'll love meeting Ursula's little Aiden. Just bring yourself and Aiden, Ursula. I'm sure we don't need any more food. Mom went into town today with a huge grocery list."

That settled, Whitney and Edward turned to walk the mile back to the beach with Ms. Ellie following. They turned to wave good-bye however, their friend was no longer in sight.

Edward's arm felt so much better they walked back much quicker than they'd gone out and soon drew near to the spot where he'd left the bike. At first, they didn't see it. Extremely upset, Edward looked frantically in all directions, then shouted, "There it is! Up by the trees! How did that happen?"

Reaching his bike, Edward stopped in his tracks to stare. "This can't be my bike!" But there was the decal of New Zealand's Flag he'd stuck on the handlebar. "This is my bike, but it can't be! It looks better than it did before the accident! There's not a scratch on it!" Edward and Whitney stared at the beautiful bike a minute longer, then looked at each other and yelled, "Ursula!" at the same time. Pretty certain they'd just solved the mystery, they waved good-bye, and headed in opposite directions.

Grinning at how badly this day had begun, yet how well it had ended, Whitney's opinion about tomorrow's BBQ had changed. She looked forward to it now and thought, "Yep, Mallory's older brother wasn't such a cranky biker boy after all." Feeling more lighthearted than she had in a month, she whistled all the way up the long flight of stairs to the house. Opening the back door, she yelled, "Mom we're home!"

# Chapter Sixteen

# A MYSTERIOUS FOG

Whitney woke to the sound of rain softly taping against her window. Opening one eye, she looked at her clock. "Wow, I can't believe it's 11:00 already! I never sleep this late!" Stretching, she threw her covers off and inspected her ankle. It was no longer swollen, and the black and blue bruises were barely visible. Stunned at how quickly it was healing, she smiled knowingly, "It must be the magic of Yagdi!" Walking to her window, she saw low gray clouds completely covering the sky, and they sure looked like they carried lots of rain. "It doesn't look like a beach day. No flip-flops or beach bag for me today." Putting on pants and a long-sleeved T-Shirt, she tucked her necklace under her shirt, and headed downstairs.

Her mom was on the phone with Edward's grandparents as she walked into the kitchen. Surprised she felt so lazy, she rubbed her eyes and poured some orange juice then sat down to wait for her mom to finish her conversation.

Susan finally hung up and grinned at her daughter. "Good afternoon, dear daughter! This rainy day certainly allowed you to sleep in!"

Whitney mumbled, "Morning mom." Putting down her orange juice, she said, "I can't believe I did that. It must be the gloomy day. How are Edward's grandparents doing?"

"We just postponed the BBQ until tomorrow. I checked the weather and it's supposed to rain all day and into the night with possible thunderstorms. Looks like a good day to read and work on our puzzle by the fire. Unfortunately, one of us has to get back to work. Enjoy your quiet day!" Waving, she headed down the hall to her clinic, coffee in hand.

Whitney thought that sounded just about perfect and admitted she was grateful to have a down day all to herself. She had a lot of confusing thoughts to sort through.

The rain continued all day as predicted, so she worked on their puzzle and wrote a letter to her friend. She admitted to Mallory that her biker brother wasn't as bad as she'd expected, and she'd actually discovered some redeeming qualities. Knowing Mallory would get a kick out of hearing how they'd met, she described their collision on the beach using great detail. She also told her friend how irritating her brother was when he blamed her for his accident. She purposefully left out the part where his bike had been miraculously fixed. In fact, Whitney realized there was a lot about that day she couldn't share with her pen pal and that was upsetting in so many ways.

Late in the afternoon, Whitney wrapped herself in a blanket and sat down by the fire with a book. She felt so relaxed and marveled at how good it felt to have a "day off" and admitted, "There haven't been enough days like this lately!"

When she finished working, Susan peeked in the living room and found her daughter sound asleep in front of the fireplace. The fire had died down and only a few hot red embers remained, so the room was quite chilly. A blanket was spread across her legs with a book about 'Dragon Folklore' laying on top.

Susan picked up the book and noticed it was open to a section about the mannerisms of baby dragons. Smiling, but not surprised, at her imaginative daughter's choice of reading material, she closed the book and put it aside. Drawing the blanket up to her daughter's chin, she threw some small logs onto the hot coals, knowing the red embers would soon catch them on fire.

It was time for dinner, but just as she walked into the kitchen, lightening lit up the sky and thunder rumbled loudly overhead. They'd experienced many storms while living on Lake Superior, and that one sounded very close. Susan held her breath when the lights flickered but stayed on. "Thank goodness!" she murmured.

Dinner could wait until after they watched the storm. They loved doing that from their screened in porch because it offered a spectacular view of Lake Superior! On her way to the porch, Susan discovered her daughter was awake and stretching, so she motioned for Whitney to follow her.

Hearing the rain pounding on their roof, Whitney realized there was a storm to watch. Stretching one more time, she jumped up and followed her mom. The lightning was indeed putting on quite a show as they settled into comfortable chairs with deep cushions designed to sink into. Snuggling in, Whitney brought her legs up under her and prepared to enjoy the show. Susan grinned at her daughter, then did the same thing. Both looked out the window in anticipation, always thrilled by Mother Nature's incredible performance.

It was still daylight, but the dark ominous thunderclouds made it look like night had fallen. Each bolt of lightning momentarily illuminated the lake's churning waters far below. Huge waves crashed onto shore, bringing treasures from the depths of the lake to scatter across the beach, before receding back into the dark waters. "Mom, tomorrow's rock hounding is going to be amazing!"

Another huge display of lightning brightened the dark sky, and Whitney warned, "Here we go!" Sure enough, a loud "Kaboom!" exploded almost immediately, powerful enough to rattle the windows. Both of them jumped, then grinned sheepishly at such a silly reaction. Whitney had counted barely a second between the lightning and its thunder, so she knew the storm was right on top of them.

The howling wind became so loud, Whitney and her mom could no longer hear the roar of the monstrous waves. The sky grew suddenly darker and had a green tint. That only happened in the most violent storms. A thick bank of dense fog suddenly rolled into view and moved slowly toward them. With eerie determination, it seemed to swallow the lake in its slow ominous approach and they both began to feel a sense of dread.

Whitney gasped when she realized why the fog felt so threatening. The mist on Yagdi looked just like this and the terrifying images of those horrid, red-eyed creatures returned. Sensing the approach of something dangerous, she wrapped the soft woolen blanket tightly around herself, as if it were a shield.

Her mom shared Whitney's feeling that something wasn't quite right and scooted her chair closer to her daughter. Wrapping herself in a blanket just as her daughter had done, she grabbed Whitney's hand and admitted, "This storm has the same fury and power as the last one. We were lucky last time, and the lights never went out. Let's hope our luck continues tonight."

They watched the fog wrap its spindly fingers around their house. Slithering through the small holes in the porch screens, its persistence felt somehow intrusive. The strange mist seemed to be looking for any little crack or crevice that would allow it to enter their home. Feeling a sudden chill, Whitney shivered and felt her mom's grip tighten. Glancing at her, Whitney noticed she was frowning while she stared intently at the fog.

"What if the mist creatures from Yagdi had actually figured out how to enter my world? Oh man, this is a whole other twist to the spooky-acting fog!" Whitney thought as she nervously chewed on her thumbnail.

Just then an unnatural movement caught their attention. Inside the dense fog, a gray figure emerged and appeared to dance with the waving tendrils of mist. Their concern deepened the longer they watched. Whatever it was, that thing and the fog appeared to move as one, swaying side-to-side and up-and-down. Whitney began to shake uncontrollably, frightened by the dancing apparition. She tried to see further into the fog, afraid the mist creatures were hiding somewhere in there.

Susan was concerned when her daughter's face became pasty white and she started to shiver. Scooting even closer, she wrapped her arms around Whitney and hugged her close. Leaning toward her, she whispered, "Would you like to move into the kitchen with its cheerful bright light?" Whitney shook her head slowly and continued staring at the strange movements. Although very concerned about her daughter's reaction to the fog, Susan didn't say anything more. She just sat there with her arms around her daughter.

Suddenly, a very wrinkled face with a long, pointed nose and spectacles that covered very bright, very big brown eyes, slowly appeared. The face was followed shortly by a rather tall slender body.

Whitney and Susan just looked at each other and shook their heads, at a loss for words. Susan whispered, "Of course that can't be a woman walking through the fog! Our eyes must be playing tricks on us."

However, as much as they wished it was some kind of an illusion, someone or something was definitely walking toward their house. They watched in fascination as the fog wrapped itself more tightly around the figure as it moved closer to them, as if it didn't want her to leave its embrace.

Whitney nervously asked, "What on earth is an older woman doing out on such a stormy night, and without a coat or an umbrella? It's as if she rode the storm itself right to our house. This is crazy!"

Her mom was so transfixed, she didn't appear to hear her. Feeling terribly nervous, Whitney suddenly remembered her necklace and thought, "This is frightening both of us! But my stones aren't hot, so am I just imagining there's a threat somewhere in that fog?"

It took repetitive and increasingly demanding knocks on the door before either Whitney or her mom moved. Strangely, Ms. Ellie had gone to the door and seemed eager to greet their unexpected visitor. This was puzzling and very much out of character for their cautious cat. Whitney looked over toward her mom and noticed her face looked whiter than normal as she stared at their door.

"Mom, what should we do?" Whitney asked nervously.

Susan squared her shoulders, fought back her fear, and marched to the door. "Yay, mom! I'm right behind you!" Whitney cheered.

Moving to their front door, Susan kept her daughter protectively behind her. Cracking the door open just enough to peek out, both mother and daughter were shocked when they recognized the woman standing on the porch.

Susan wasn't concerned for their safety any longer, so she opened the door wide and stared into the face of the woman they'd bought their home from! Whitney's fear disappeared, replaced by the revelation that this woman looked very much like someone she'd just met.

Noticing the same inquisitive look on her mom's face, Whitney whispered, "Mom, do you think she looks like someone else?" When she saw her mom's almost imperceptible nod, she knew they'd be having an interesting discussion later.

After an awkward greeting, Susan motioned for their visitor to come in. They hadn't seen Clara since they'd bought her house. Her friendly face still held sparkling brown eyes, a very big, pointed nose, and a large ear-to-ear grin. She was tall and slender with very long fingers. In irritation, she used them to push her glasses back into position as she walked through the doorway.

Smiling warmly at each of them, Clara glanced around the

kitchen. She seemed genuinely happy to see them, and very pleased to be back in her old house. However, she was soaked, and water from her hair was dripping onto a very red face. Susan's became concerned for the poor woman out on such an awful night.

Bursting into action, she ushered Clara to a chair at the table saying, "This is an unexpected surprise, but you do look wet and you must be terribly chilled. Let me get you a towel to dry off some of that dampness," and rushed away, leaving Whitney alone with Clara.

As soon as her mom left the room, Clara looked at Whitney and transformed into Ursula, then back to Clara again. It all happened so fast, all Whitney could do was sit down in the nearest chair, completely dumbfounded. Finally finding her voice, she asked, "What just happened?"

Ursula glanced in the direction Susan had just gone and said in a low secretive voice, "I have to talk quickly because I know your mother will return shortly. Things have really begun heating up on Yagdi. Our enemies have become bolder and more capable at carrying out their ever-increasing devious plans. You were wise to fear that fog, Whitney. The Mist Creatures figured out how to use it as a bridge to get to you. I sensed it happening and came as quickly as I could to ensure your safety. My appearance sent them scurrying back where they belong, but I'll stay a short while to be absolutely sure they don't try to return. Follow my lead with your mother, Okay?" and winked.

Shocked by this unexpected turn of events, Whitney just nodded. However, she was grateful for her friend's timely intervention. Moving closer, Whitney said conspiratorially, "Honestly, I was really afraid. I somehow knew they were near. Something was actually bothering mom too. I'm glad you're here, Ursula." Laughing, Whitney asked, "Or should I call you Clara?"

Susan returned and asked, "What's so funny, you two?" as she handed Clara the towel.

Drying off quickly, Clara said, "Thank you for the towel, Susan. My it's wet out there!" Then she explained, "I was just telling Whitney about my wild ride through this crazy storm tonight. It's been quite an adventure. It was worth it, though. It's so good to see you both again!" and gave them big enthusiastic bear hugs. Then she bent over to pet Ms. Ellie, who was purring loudly as she strutted, tail high, in and out of their guest's legs.

"I'm sorry I missed hearing about your stormy adventure. Maybe you can tell it again later? Anyway, it's good to see you again too, Clara!"

Walking to the cupboard to grab three mugs, she continued, "Some hot cocoa should do us all good!"

That prompted excited clapping and an enthusiastic, "Yes, Please!" from Clara.

As Whitney stirred the milk on the stove, Clara said, "It's so nice to be back here for a visit. You both seem happy living here, something I knew would be true the moment I saw you both at my door."

Whitney was just about to respond when her mom broke in, "We love it here, don't we Whitney. But how about we drink our cocoa in front of the fireplace? It's so much cozier." Looking pointedly at their guest's very red hands, she continued, "It certainly appears you need to warm up those hands, Clara."

Susan directed Clara to the large, overstuffed chair closest to the warming fire, and watched their elderly guest ease herself into the chair, gripping the arms for support. When she almost disappeared in the soft cushions, Susan said with amusement, "That chair seems to have swallowed you up, Clara!"

When she joined them a few minute later, Whitney noticed Clara had perched herself on the edge of her chair to hold her hands close to the fire and Ms. Ellie was laying comfortably at her feet. Her mom had settled into the chair next to Clara. Looking up at her daughter, she shrugged her shoulders with a secretive look Whitney interpreted as, "What on earth is going on?"

She handed a warm steaming mug of cocoa and a chocolate chip cookie to her mom, then waited for Clara to settle back against the cushions before passing a mug and cookie to her. Carrying her own to her beanbag chair, Whitney plopped down saying, "I see Ms. Ellie's found a friend." Clara just grinned and held the warm mug between her cold hands.

For a short while, they all gazed into the fire enjoying the delicious warmth of their cocoa and every bite of their cookie. Suddenly, Whitney's mom blurted out, "I missed your story earlier, so may I ask what you're doing out in a storm like this?"

Smiling gleefully, Clara answered, "Why, challenging as they tend to be, stormy nights like this are my favorite nights to be out riding around."

Thinking her explanation was odd, Susan grew more curious. "Riding around in what? I didn't see a car, bicycle or any other form of transportation. How did you get here, Clara?"

Dying to hear how her friend would answer that question, Whitney grinned into her cocoa as her mom politely allowed their visitor time to take a few more sips of her cocoa. However, she could tell her mom's impatience was growing with each passing minute. Clara certainly didn't seem to be in a hurry to answer. She looked quite content just gazing into the fire and petting Ms. Ellie.

Sipping on her cocoa, she wondered how best to answer Susan's question. Not wanting to reveal too much, she simply answered, "I was dropped off and will be picked up when I'm ready to move on."

Carefully watching her mom's reaction to Clara's vague answer, Whitney knew she wasn't satisfied. In fact, she looked a little put off but simply shrugged her shoulders again. "Way to go, mom!" Whitney thought taking another sip of her cocoa, glad she'd apparently decided to drop it.

Clearing her throat, Susan continued quietly, "We sure did enjoy meeting you. The day we accidentally discovered your 'For Sale' sign, it was almost hidden in weeds at the end of the driveway. We weren't even sure it was still for sale. However, you graciously ushered us in and gave us the grand tour. You called it such an endearing name, 'Travellers Rest.' It seemed like it fit the house perfectly, but I always wondered what prompted such an unusual name?"

Clara's eyes sparkled and she answered, "I like the name 'Traveller.' I love to travel so much that it seemed appropriate. Travelling gives one energy, don't you think? It's so exciting!"

Hearing another vague response, Susan decided she wouldn't let it go this time. Prodding for more information she continued, "That makes a bit of sense. But you also said something like, 'We've been waiting a long time to find you.' I hope you don't think my question intrusive, but I've always wondered what was meant by that. Who was 'we'? If I remember correctly, you lived here alone."

"I don't ever take offense from intelligent questions, even when they're a bit misguided." Clara said, "I'm enjoying our time immensely and hope you are too. I was in the area, and just had to see how you were both doing."

Looking at Susan, she continued, "To answer your question, when I sold this house to you, I was indeed living alone. I also knew my home needed a family to shelter. That's why I was so happy when you both came along. I can see it was a perfect match and that makes me quite pleased."

Not finished with her polite grilling of their guest, Susan said somewhat apologetically, "I promise this is my last question. Actually, it's more of an observation than a question. I think you look very much like a sweet woman named Ursula we met just the other day. You're considerably taller and slimmer, but your mannerisms and sparkling brown eyes are identical. The similarities are uncanny!"

Almost choking on her cocoa, Whitney looked at Ursula with intense curiosity. How was she going to navigate her mom's astute observation?

Tilting her head as if thinking, Clara cleared her throat and giggled, "Looks can be so terribly deceiving, can't they? I often have strangers come up to me thinking I look like someone they know."

Raising one eyebrow at Whitney, she turned toward Susan and finished, "I'm never who they think I am. The truth is, we are seldom who we appear to be."

Mystified, Susan became silent and chewed on her lower lip as she contemplated the strange events from this night, and their even stranger guest. The rest of the evening was spent talking about the house. They gave Clara a tour through the house, and Susan's vet clinic, to show her the changes they'd made. Many times, Susan reassured the former owner that it was a perfect home for her and Whitney.

After the tour, someone's stomach growled almost as loud as the rumble of thunder outside. When Susan asked Clara if she'd like to stay for a home-cooked fish dinner, Whitney thought she looked quite tempted. Her eyes brightened, and she could have sworn her mouth watered.

However, Clara declined the invitation saying, "Thank you for such a generous invitation, but I really must be headed home." Just then Whitney heard a boom of thunder, as if in agreement with their guest's decision.

At the door, their surprise visitor bent down once again to pet Ms. Ellie and said, "Now you take good care of Whitney and her mom. They're both very special to me." Rising, she gave each of them one last bear hug and opened the door.

Whitney and her mother watched the fog greet Clara and wrap itself around their unexpected visitor, as if it had been waiting for her return. Her body seemed to dissolve into the fog, then disappeared completely. Shaking her head, Whitney's mother sighed and said, "What a very strange woman Clara is!" then turned toward the kitchen to prepare their very late dinner.

Whitney remained at the door, staring into the fog where Clara had just disappeared. Overwhelmed by the speed at which her life was changing, she was feeling a hint of fear mixed with sadness when a very loud "Kaboom!" rattled the rooftop making her jump.

Suddenly remembering the reason for Ursula's impromptu visit, she peered into the fog, hoping she wouldn't see those evil red eyes. Shivering, she put her hand up to slam the door shut when she heard a loud call pierce the dense fog. It sounded far away, so she suspected it was a ship's foghorn. Then she saw a figure moving deep inside the bank of fog. Clara turned her way and waved than began to run. Whitney waved back as Clara transformed back into her true self. In seconds, she'd become Traveller, the magnificent polar bear just as the fog began to disappear into the low bank of clouds.

# Chapter Seventeen

# A CURIOUS INVITATION

Whitney squinted at the bright sunlight streaming through her window. It appeared to be encouraging her to get out of bed. Ms. Ellie was nowhere in sight. Amazed she'd slept in once again she ran to the window to check the weather. Seeing blue skies with no hint of clouds, she smiled thinking, "It's going to be a perfect day for a BBQ with friends."

Walking into the kitchen, she noticed Ms. Ellie was pacing back and forth rather impatiently, occasionally stopping to look into her empty food dish, while her mom talked on the phone. It appeared to be an important call because her mom put a finger to her mouth as she walked in.

Trying to figure out what was going on, she listened carefully, but the one-sided conversation didn't tell her much. Her mom said things like, "That's interesting; I feel honored," or "How many days did you say?" When she finally hung up, she shook her head then twirled around to look at her daughter with sparkling eyes and a big smile.

"I've just been invited to speak at the annual National Veterinary Science Symposium in Denver, Colorado. They want me to talk about my practice because I chose to work in a rural area. They recognize that's an area that's underserved and want me to talk about my life as a rural veterinarian, particularly in the Upper Peninsula of Michigan. They're hoping my speech and follow up workshops will encourage graduating veterinarians to follow my lead."

Whitney stared at her mother for a few seconds, then ran to hug her announcing, "You have to do this, mom. They'll learn so much from you! When is it?"

Looking sheepish, her mom answered, "That's the problem. It's in two days. I can't leave you alone, but it's such short notice to try to find someone. My first choice would be for you to come along, Whitney. I know I'd be stuck at the conference most of the day, but we'd still have plenty of time to go out on the town shopping. We could take drives into the mountains for hikes and picnics. What do you think?"

Whitney thought long and hard but decided she really wanted to stay home. Her life had become pretty exciting, and she didn't want to miss any of it! It felt like there were important things left to be discussed with Traveller, or Ursula, whoever she decided to be at the moment. She enjoyed spending time with either one of them. Then there was her new biker friend who was beginning to grow on her.

Susan noticed her daughter's hesitation, and said, "I can see you'd rather stay home, and I can't say I blame you as busy as I'll be. However, I can't leave you here by yourself. You'd probably be just fine, but that's not an option. I'm sorry, Whitney."

Seeing the fierce protectiveness in her mom's eyes, Whitney knew arguing would be pointless, so she threw out another idea. "Mom, what about Ursula? She's such a sweet lady and I really enjoy her company. She and little Aidan would keep Ellie and me hopping the entire time you're gone. She's got more energy than a person half her age!" She dropped it to allow her mom time to consider her idea and eat breakfast.

Susan called all of her upcoming appointments and resched-uled each one, patiently explaining her exciting opportunity. Finished with her last call, Susan put the phone down and looked at her daughter. "You may be onto something, Whitney. Ursula did seem very sweet. However, I'm a little confused why she disappeared that day in the jewelry store, and poor Randolph didn't have a clue who she might have been."

Whitney tried to think of something that might make sense, and not be an outright lie. "I forgot to tell you. I ran into Ursula out on the point and spent the afternoon with her. I asked her that very same question." Then she repeated what Ursula had told her. She knew it couldn't ring completely true with Susan because it hadn't with her. She just hoped it would be enough to satisfy her mom.

It did seem to work because when she was finished, Susan admitted in relief, "I knew there had to be a reasonable explanation. She was so sweet! I'll bring it up at the BBQ tonight, OK?" Suddenly very excited to spend a week with Ursula, Whitney grinned and raced over to give her mom a huge hug.

There was a lot to do to get ready for the BBQ. They set little tiki lights around the railing of the deck, opened the deep peach colored umbrella over the table, and cut some flowers, putting them into vases to place around the deck. Their purples and bright pinks made everything look so festive. As her mom cleaned the grill and made sure there was enough propane to cook the burgers, Whitney cleaned the house, just in case any of their guests made their way inside.

The day flew by and all too soon, it was time to get themselves ready. They both put on summer dresses and sandals, then Whitney's mom took two flowers from a vase to weave into their hair. Ready for their company, they went to the back deck, lit the tiki lights and sat down to watch the sun move closer to the horizon.

Hearing a "Yoo-Hoo!" they both looked toward the beach. There was Ursula waving enthusiastically up at them from the base of their stairway.

"Hi Ursula," Whitney's mom yelled waving. "Do you need assistance up the stairs? It's a long way!" Hearing Susan's sweet welcoming voice, the little dragon at Ursula's feet got so excited he started spinning in circles trying to catch his tail making Whitney and her mom laugh.

Ursula shouted back, "Oh my no, I welcome the exercise!" and began a fast walk up the stairs, navigating them with no problem. Before too long she was in front of them, smiling happily.

Hugging them enthusiastically, Ursula thanked Susan profusely for inviting them. Looking down at Aiden with his huge, adorable grin, she cooed, "Who do we have here?"

Hurrying to introduce Aiden to Susan, Whitney and Ursula both bent over and collided. Standing up quickly, rubbing their sore heads and grimacing, Ursula winked at Whitney and groaned playfully, "You have quite a hard head, young Whitney!" then picked up her little dragon.

Holding out her arms, Susan asked, "I hope you're both okay! What's this cute little puppy's name? May I hold him?"

Smiling, Ursula passed the little dragon to Susan and answered, "I'm sure we'll both be fine. This sweet little boy's name is Aiden. I've only had him a short time, but I'm already in love. His first family sadly couldn't keep him any longer, so they asked me if I would like to become his mom. They gave me the records of all his puppy shots and veterinary exams, so Aiden and I won't be needing a vet for another year. Rumor has it you're quite an outstanding veterinarian, Susan, so I'd love for you to be his new vet. That is, if you have room for one more."

Beaming at the compliment, Susan wondered about that family. Why had they taken such good care of Aiden, just to give him away? What could possibly have prompted that? They'd apparently invested a lot of time and money into their new puppy, and he was so cute!

When Susan hugged him closer, Aiden just melted into her

arms and Susan purred into his big ear, "Aww you're just too cute for your own good." Then she asked Ursula, "He's so small, but he has huge feet. That means he'll probably get quite large. What kind of puppy is he?"

Ursula shrugged her shoulders and said, "The official puppy papers just said, 'Large Mixed Breed.' I'm currently looking for a bigger house with a yard so he can grow up running free."

As soon as Susan put him back on the ground, Ms. Ellie leaped on Aiden. Wriggling free, he scooted down the stairs to the beach, missing several of the steps in his hurry to get to the bottom with their cat following close behind. The two 'kids' ran in circles and took turns chasing each other, only to race back up the stairs to do it all over again.

Susan was glad to see how well Ms. Ellie and the puppy were getting along. Then she noticed Whitney's carefree expression as she and Ursula smiled and laughed together. Having finally made a difficult decision, she took a deep breath and said, "Ursula, could I speak with you in the house for a minute?"

Watching them walk away arm in arm like old friends, Whitney grinned at how easy it was for Ursula to befriend everyone and adjust to any situation. Just then Ms. Ellie bumped into her legs trying to dodge the little dragon. Laughing, she bent over and grabbed her cat. Hugging her close, she whispered, "You're having way too much fun!"

To taunt his captive friend, Aiden looked up with his big goofy grin and cocked his head to the side, then turned in three fast circles. Knowing a dare when she saw one, the Bombay cat wriggled insistently, forcing Whitney to put her down. As soon as her small paws hit the ground, it was game on. They ran back down the stairs, ignoring most of them in their frantic race to the bottom. Instead of running back up, however, they ran toward something further down the beach.

Using her hand to shade her eyes from the glare of the setting sun, she saw who they were racing toward. Two elderly figures were walking leisurely toward her, stopping occasionally to inspect rocks that caught their eye. It had to be Edward's grandparents, but where was Edward?

More disappointed than she wanted to admit, she tried to dismiss the fact she'd been looking forward to seeing him again. Waving to catch their attention, they finally looked up and waved back. Picking up their pace, they were at the base of the stairs leading to their deck in no time.

Edward's grandpa was carrying a big pot of baked beans, and his grandma carried a small cooler with their drinks. Whitney ran down to hug each of them, then helped them carry things up to the deck.

Walking up the stairs, Edward's grandpa grew a bit out of breath, however he managed to huff out a short sentence explaining the absence of their grandson. "Edward wanted to get in a quick training session, but promised he'd join us later."

Whitney's happiness at that news erupted into a huge grin they couldn't help but notice. Although they were very interested in how their grumpy grandson had earned the interest of this sweet girl, they wisely kept that question to themselves.

They arrived on the deck just as her mom and Ursula walked out of the house. Susan looked quite pleased and Ursula was beaming. Not able to wait another moment, Ursula clapped her hands and announced, "Well Whitney, it looks like we're going to be roommates for a week." To confirm that, Whitney looked at her mom and saw her smile and nod.

She shrieked, "You get to go to your conference, mom! I'm so excited for you and I know you'll be amazing! And Ursula, you and I'll have so much fun!"

Happy to see her daughter's excitement, Susan went over to Edward's grandparents to welcome them. Taking their pot of beans, she motioned for them to sit at the table. Pulling their iced tea out of the cooler, the grandparents grabbed two festive paper cups, clinked them together saying 'cheers' and took long swigs trying to cool down from their walk.

Whitney was pouring lemonade for her mom when she saw biker boy riding down the beach in their direction. Edward's arrival brought chaos to the deck as both Aiden and Ms. Ellie vied for his attention. When he got down on his knees to give each a proper hello, their excitement erupted, almost knocking the poor kid over with their enthusiastic greeting.

As they ran off to find another exciting game, Edward was able to stand up. He stuck out his hand and grinned politely at Whitney's mom. "Some entrance, huh. Hi, I'm Edward. It's so nice to meet you," then smiled at Whitney. His interaction with the two goofballs had earned Susan's instant approval, so she gave him a very welcoming smile and shook his hand.

With introductions behind them, everyone sat back to enjoy the evening. Edward offered to flip the burgers, which freed Susan to run between their guests and the kitchen, chatting easily with Ursula and Edward's grandparents.

Joining Edward, Whitney said, "Hey Biker Boy. Glad you could join us. Looks like my mom approves of you. She's such an animal lover and notices when other humans feel the same way. And thanks for taking over the burgers for her. It allowed her to play hostess and talk to everyone. Tell me about this competition you're in later this summer."

They stood there talking, unaware there were four pairs of eyes watching their easy friendship with a great deal of interest. Susan really liked Whitney's new friend and was happy to see her with someone her own age. Living out here, they didn't have families living nearby, so Whitney was pretty much on her own while she worked every day.

At the same time, Edward's grandparents looked at each other shaking their heads. His grandma whispered, "What happened to our grumpy grandson?" All he could offer was a discrete shrug of his shoulders. Ursula, however, was beyond excited. She smiled in their direction and thought to herself, "This is working out so much better than I'd hoped!"

The delicious smell of hamburgers being grilled had made them all hungry, so when Edward yelled, "Burgers up!" No one needed a second invitation and jumped up to load their plates. Sitting back down, they were preparing to dive into their feast when Susan stopped them to make a quick announcement. "As you may or may not know, I'm a vet, and my clinic is right here in our house. I've just been asked to speak at a National Symposium for Veterinary Science in two days."

At their claps and whistles, she bowed good naturedly and continued, "I'm thrilled and honored beyond belief. However, I'm only able to go because of Ursula. She's agreed to stay here with Whitney for the week I'll be gone." Clapping erupted once again, and a very pleased Ursula jumped up to bow dramatically low while sweeping her arm out.

Susan raised her glass of lemonade, waited for everyone to join her, then toasted, "Here's to new friends!" prompting yet another round of cheers and glasses held high.

The mood for the evening turned very festive, with a little help from the two hilarious 'kids,' and everyone had a memorable night. As they were all leaving, they promised to do it again. Edward's grandma admitted it would have to be soon explaining, "Unfortunately, we'll be leaving when the forest campground closes for the season."

Never one to miss an opportunity, Ursula used their announcement to solidify her plan to keep the kids and little Aiden together. Turning to her two new friends she said, "You know I just heard about a house in town that's available now. The owners needed to leave earlier than they'd planned, and they'd love to have someone rent their home while they're gone. If you're interested, I'll give you their phone number." Surprised and pleased, they nodded and took the number from their new friend.

Bringing out their flashlights, Edward and his grandparents said good night and headed back to the campground. Before they left, Whitney noticed Ursula and Edward were involved in what seemed like a very serious conversation. Curious what it might have been about, she made a mental note to find out.

Ursula waved good-bye a short while later and made her way down the stairs with Aiden in her arms. Whitney and her mom watched her until her twinkling flashlight was just a tiny speck far down the beach.

Smiling at each other, Susan put an arm around her daughter's shoulder and said, "That was fun. What a nice group of people. I really like Ursula! And Whitney, you and Edward seemed to hit it off well indeed. He sure doesn't seem like the kid Mallory describes, does he?" Seeing Whitney's shrug, she dropped it for the time being. They both turned toward the messy tables, groaned then began cleaning up.

# Chapter Eighteen

# MERGAN ARRIVES!

The next two days were a flurry of activity as Susan got ready for her trip. She'd spent hours preparing her speech, doing laundry and packing.

The evening before Susan's early morning departure, Ursula and Aiden arrived and made themselves at home in the spare bedroom. After settling in, she offered to help. "Helping you get ready would be a good way to get the lay of the land."

Whitney smiled at her friend's strange phrases. Susan was grateful for her offer and found plenty of last-minute projects. Finally, everything was done, and Susan was packed and ready for her trip.

They sat in front of the fireplace working on the puzzle with Susan dominating the conversation. She excitedly described what she'd be talking about and was over the moon excited for the opportunity. When everyone started yawning, they said good night and headed to their bedrooms.

Susan left first thing in the morning, with the sun barely peeking over the horizon. Coffee in her hand, she leaned over to kiss her daughter and whispered, "We'll talk every day, but if something goes terribly wrong, please call me right away. I can be home in a few short hours! Stay safe and happy, Whitney!"

Whitney smiled proudly at her mother. "We'll be fine, mom. Knock 'em dead! I'll miss you and I love you!" Hugging her daughter, Susan whispered back, "Love you more!" Getting in the car, she paused to wave once again then drove out of sight.

Ursula clapped her hands and announced, "OK, Whitney. Let's have a big breakfast because you'll be needing it!"

Looking at her roommate in surprise, she asked, "What do you mean by that?"

Grinning, Ursula motioned Whitney back into the house then into the kitchen and said, "I'll explain everything while we eat."

As they entered the kitchen, Whitney heard a knock on the back door. Wondering who that could possibly be this early, she went to open it mumbling, "I just wanted to go back to bed for a couple of hours." Rubbing her eyes, she opened the door to find Edward standing there looking every bit as tired as she felt. Instantly suspicious, she looked at Ursula then back at Edward.

Whitney's questions began as Biker Dude make his way into the kitchen. "OK, you two, spill it! I saw you talking about something pretty serious at the BBQ. Does this early morning gathering have anything to do with that? Whatever's going on, why wasn't I aware of it?"

Looking at each of them in turn, Ursula simply answered, "All in good time, dear. Breakfast will be served in just a few minutes, so why don't you both have a seat at the table. While we eat, we can discuss the week ahead of us."

Whitney and Edward looked at each other, shrugged their shoulders then did as they were told. Aiden and Ms. Ellie moved to their places under the table, their mouths watering in anticipation of dropped food that was sure to come.

Shoving heaping plates of pancakes and eggs in front of them, Ursula sat down and announced, "Eat hearty because this week is going to be filled with what I like to call intense training. I imagine it will be much like Edward's training for his triathlon. By the way, dear, I must say that training is going to give you an edge over Whitney as we get started."

Grinning at Whitney, Edward taunted his friend, "Hear that Whitney? Looks like you've got some catching up to do!"

Outraged at the mere thought he could beat her in anything, Whitney accepted the challenge saying, "Just give it your best, because you'll be needing it, Biker Boy!" which brought enthusiastic laughing from both Ursula and Edward.

The little dragon joined in with a very strange half bark-half shriek, causing everyone, including the cat, to look curiously at him. Opening his mouth, the little dragon repeated it more loudly and grinned. Whitney said, "What a strange little guy, but so totally irresistible. You sound like a teenage boy whose voice is changing. Maybe this is a sign you're growing up, little guy!" and grinned back.

Clearing her throat Ursula said, "That is probably very true, young Whitney," and looked more closely at the little dragon under the table. "By the way, I'm so happy for your mom. What an incredible and well-deserved opportunity she's been given, and so out of the blue. I'm thrilled to be here while she's gone because I must say the timing couldn't be more perfect to begin your training."

Ignoring their puzzled looks, she rambled on. "Normally, it's a very long journey from Yagdi to Earth, however my friend Mergan will be able to use my portal, now that it's back in operation." Stopping to take a breath, she ignored their confusion and continued, "Times are rather dangerous right now, so he's the only other being I've entrusted to use it without my presence. Anyway, regardless of the convenient travel to your world, I'm certain my dear friend will need proper nourishment before we begin. I should forewarn you he's very driven so I'm sure he'll want to commence with training immediately. He's quite passionate about what he does and is very well aware time is of the essence."

Noticing their frowns had deepened, Ursula explained, "Mergan is considered a mage in our world. He's quite old and very wise and his abilities are truly remarkable. His reputation is so well known, Yagdian kids sing songs about the mage and pretend to be him by using sticks they find laying around the schoolyard. He's quite proficient at helping folks discover their unique talents.

Once that's accomplished, he expertly trains them to use those skills. In fact, he was my mentor many years ago."

After a moment of stunned silence, Edward blurted out, "Ursula, I want to train with Mergan, and I want to help the citizens of Yagdi, but I don't know about the timing. My focus has got to be on training for the triathlon. I'm not sure I can take so much time away from that right now, Ursula." Feeling sorry for him, Whitney looked to their friend to hear her answer.

Smiling, Ursula explained patiently, "Young Edward, this training will be unlike anything you've ever experienced. I promise you it will be an outstanding way to train for your event." Not convinced, Edward decided to let it go for the time being and see how things progressed.

As if on cue, a loud banging at the back door with some kind of stick made them all jump. "Mergan's here," Ursula giggled, and ran to let her friend in.

Blowing into the kitchen like a full-blown thunderstorm, the mage announced in a booming voice, "That Portal of yours comes in mighty handy, Ursula! I assume you have it effectively concealed from our enemies!"

Whitney could feel the energy radiating out of this stranger, both natural and unnatural, and it was making her nervous. His eyebrows were huge and bushy and the eyes below them were strikingly blue. Although rather thin, the mage carried himself with an air of extreme confidence.

Striding to the girl with long efficient steps, the mage put out his hand saying, "It's wonderful to meet you, young chosen one." Perceiving her hesitation, he smiled and added, "Don't worry, I don't bite!"

His piercing gaze held her uncomfortably captive, and Whitney noticed the man's smile didn't quite reach his eyes. In fact, it seemed awkward and unpracticed, as if rarely used. However, he was a friend of Ursula's, so Whitney smiled weakly and, with some hesitancy, shook his hand. The wizard received an equally cautious reception from Edward.

When his stern expression landed on his former student, Whitney witnessed a miraculous transformation. A genuine smile gave a welcoming twinkle to his eyes that removed all trace of his gruff demeanor and his arms opened wide for a hug. Ursula squealed with delight, threw her arms out and ran eagerly into her old friend's arms. Stepping away, she happily told everyone to sit down.

While Whitney and Edward ate their breakfast, they followed Ursula's happy movements. She poured a steaming cup of coffee for her mentor then bustled around the kitchen, humming as she prepared another breakfast.

Turning toward the three, Ursula noticed Edward and Whitney were still frowning and trying to hide their quizzical glances toward the Wizard, while her old friend seemed oblivious to their rapt attention and was staring pensively into his mug of coffee. "They're all so dear to me!" she thought, then announced cheerfully, "This room is filled with three people who are very important to me. Whitney and Edward are the two chosen ones I've been telling you about, Mergan. They're quite remarkable indeed and if their training goes well enough, they'll become the perfect pair to protect our young Aiden."

Somewhat offended at Ursula's, "if training goes well

enough," the mage cleared his throat and said loudly, "You know better than to doubt my capabilities, Ursula. By the end of this week, I can guarantee they will be the highly trained allies we desperately need."

She had complete confidence that her dear friend would live up to his promise. However, Whitney and Edward looked quite skeptical, and were still obviously uncomfortable with the mage. Hoping to ease their concerns, she coaxed, "Mergan, why don't you begin by explaining who you are, what you do and your plans for training these two?"

The wizard thought Ursula's suggestion had some merit, but when he looked at the two kids with probing eyes and furrowed brows, he only succeeded in increasing their discomfort. With a sense of dread, Whitney and Edward glanced toward each other sympathetically, uncertain about what was to come.

Noticing their concern appeared to ramp up when Mergan looked at them, Ursula scolded her friend, "Now Mergan, shame on you. There's no need to scare these youngsters half to death. You have a very fierce looking scowl on your face right now that I think this breakfast might eliminate," and placed a huge pile of food in front of him.

Ursula was right and they were both grateful when the wizard's frightening scowl turned from them toward his plate. Ignoring all of them, the menacing man ate with a great deal of enthusiasm. Not able to talk and eat at the same time, he'd chosen to remain silent. They watched as the mage efficiently stuffed every last morsel into his mouth as quickly as possible.

With her friend distracted, Ursula seized on the opportunity to brighten the dark mood that had crept into their morning. "Dearest Whitney and Edward, please excuse my friend's rather fearsome presence. You must know it doesn't reflect on you at all. However, he takes his job very seriously and feels the success or failure of his students reflects on him. That's why he's such a remarkable sage. He doesn't accept defeat but will push you until success is imminent."

Whitney and Edward looked at each other, then toward the strange and ominous man who'd temporarily forgotten them. His head was down close to the plate because it allowed him to shovel food in as quickly as possible. Whitney discovered that her eagerness to begin training had vanished. She feared this powerful man who was supposed to guide them, and it appeared Edward felt the same way.

Finishing his huge breakfast, Mergan sat up, gave a satisfied burp and wiped his mouth with a napkin. Pushing his chair away from the table, he looked at Ursula and said, "Compliments to the chef for a mighty fine breakfast," making her beam with pride.

Noticing his presence was unintentionally frightening both Whitney and Edward, Mergan said, "How about we begin again, young Whitney and Edward. Let me reintroduce myself. I'm Mergan, and I'm here to help each of you become more than you could have ever imagined. That's something I do very well." Looking at Ursula he admitted, "However, a very dear friend of mine once said, 'The training is nothing, the will is everything.'" Her proud smile lit up the room.

Watching the kids carefully, he explained, "Your training, once Ursula and I have explained the procedure to your satisfaction, can be a remarkable success. However, I can only take you so far. The rest will be up to each of you."

Sighing, he continued, "I wish I'd been at our settlement on Yagdi the day you visited. I hear the celebration in your honor was a great success. Unfortunately, I was out chasing the bad guys, which allowed all of you to enjoy your day. I have heard very good things about you, but do you know what is most impressive to me?"

They just stared at him with shocked expressions, so Mergan continued, "What impresses me most is that you both have an overwhelming need to help others. That's a powerful force that will give your training some teeth. I want to thank you personally for running to my good friend's defense when the mist creatures launched their surprising ambush. You showed skills that, although not quite meeting your expectations, showed us what we have to work with."

Edward looked growingly concerned, and finally blurted out, "Sir, I'm training for a triathlon in just a few short weeks. I don't see how I can do both, and it's a commitment that's really important to me!"

Whitney got up the nerve to jump in next by admitting, "I really messed up that day on Yagdi. I tried to help Ursula, but nothing I did lasted long enough to do any good."

Ursula answered first, "Let me explain the why before Mergan shares the how." Seeing she had their undivided attention she dove in, "Whitney, you have a 13th birthday coming up in just two weeks, correct?" Without waiting for an answer, she kept talking. "This past month you've begun to feel things are 'spinning out of control.' Anyway, I believe that's how you described it to your mother. You have been feeling changes inside of you that you can't explain, don't want anything to do with, and wish they'd just go away. At the same time, you're interested in discovering what's causing those feelings. Am I right?"

Seeing Whitney's bewildered nod, Ursula looked toward Edward and forged ahead. "Young Edward, you've been feeling like you aren't the same person you were just a month ago. It's made you a 'grumpy brother,' according to your sister. Have I left anything out?" Edward's self-conscious shake of his head was her cue to move forward because it was time that they fully understood why their lives were changing.

"You were both born with special gifts, which is why you're considered chosen ones. Mergan will help you learn how to call on those gifts when they're required, and then use them effectively. I can promise you from first-hand experience, that will be quite rewarding indeed."

Having piqued their interest, Ursula looked directly at Whitney and continued, "Whitney dear, you are extraordinarily tenacious, loving, generous, open to new ideas, adventurous and smart. You are extremely fond of all animals, and beyond loyal to those you love." Then turning to Edward, she continued, "Edward you're stubborn, strong, loyal, loving and driven to succeed in whatever you've set out to accomplish. Your triathlon is a perfect example of that."

Looking carefully at each of them, she added, "At our celebration, you both witnessed, first-hand, how much our citizens appreciate you. They have met you both and learned of your willingness to risk your lives for our future leader and protector, little Aiden. Therefore, they now hold you in high esteem, and are thrilled to honor you."

Looking toward her mentor and friend, Ursula finished by promising, "Each of your talents will be revealed and blossom under Mergan's careful tutelage. You will become well equipped to handle any threats against Aiden or yourselves." A pleased grin erupted on Mergan's face at his student and dear friend's kind words.

"Oh, there's one last important thing I must tell you both. We are all so very sorry our enemies are now terrorizing both of you! However, I think you now realize you have powerful allies in the good defenders of Yagdi. Our mighty dragons and ferocious bear clan, which I am proud to be a part of, will be joining us. Together we'll form an extremely formidable and powerful alliance, designed to make our enemies cower in fear!"

Mergan began to clap and continued for a long while, in spite of the growing blush on his former student's face. The mage's enthusiastic appreciation for Ursula brought a lighter atmosphere into the room, and Whitney was thrilled to see a happy smile appear on her friend's sweet face.

Intrigued by the hint of a very close bond between Mergan and Ursula, Whitney leaned forward and watched their interactions carefully. Their stolen glances and smiles and noting how Ursula would frequently touch her mage's hand while she talked, made her suspect there was more to their story.

She and Edward felt themselves beginning to relax and enjoy the entertainment. As Ursula and Mergan were getting caught up, they passed their uneaten breakfast scraps to the two sweet creatures waiting eagerly under the table.

# Chapter Nineteen

# TRAINING BEGINS!

M ergan cleared his throat and began, "It looks like the why is explained. Now it's time you heard how we will proceed."

Whitney thought he looked quite gruff once again, but now it seemed far less threatening. Edward was staring at the mage expectantly, with no sign of concern. He seemed to be adjusting to all of this quite well.

"First things first," Mergan began, "I will expect complete and total commitment on your part from the moment we begin until the time I feel confident that I've shown you everything I know. At that point, it will be up to each of you to continue your own training. My services will no longer be needed. However, you will need immense and ongoing self-discipline. Isn't that correct, Ursula?"

Nodding excitedly, she added, "Mergan only has this week to work with you, while your mother is at her conference. His expertise is desperately needed on Yagdi, so at week's end, he must return. Since he has so little time, training will be necessarily intense and we must insist that you continue practicing your new skills daily, even in his absence. That's why I brought the two of you together. The more you practice, encourage and challenge each other, the more advanced your skills will become, and your confidence will soar. You must set aside other plans and commit to this endeavor for an entire week." Looking humorously at each of them she asked, "Do you think you can do that without inflicting serious harm on one another?"

Looking from her to each other, Whitney and Edward both shrugged their shoulders. She took that as a confirmation, at least for the time being. However, she'd learned much about them over the past few days. Armed with that information, Ursula wondered with a certain amount of humor how long it would take for the fireworks to erupt.

Keeping her musings to herself, Ursula clapped her hands gleefully and suggested, "Let's get started then!" Looking at the mage for agreement, she said, "How about we begin with Whitney and Edward training separately." Mergan agreed and wasted no time leading Edward down to the beach. Following his teacher out the door, Edward glanced back at Whitney with an expression she read loud and clear, "Here we go, ready or not!"

As the door shut behind them, Ursula looked at Whitney and quickly explained her goals for their week together. "It's very important that we discover all of your gifts as soon as we possibly can. Then we can begin to practice how best to use them. We all want to protect little Aiden, but it's critical you stay safe from harm as well, so you and Edward must learn to work as a team. Together, you will be formidable indeed, especially with Ms. Ellie as your backup. She is well aware that her job is extremely critical. She'll watch over all of you and become her true self if and when any of you are threatened."

Seeing that she'd made Whitney uneasy with her business-like manner, Ursula smiled reassuringly and admitted, "You and Edward will be amazing, and I know you'll learn quickly. I have no doubt whatsoever Aiden will be in very capable hands."

When a small smile appeared on Whitney's face, she continued, "If I can create a life-or-death scenario that's threatening enough to coax your protective instincts into action, the gifts hidden inside of you will break free. At that moment, your destiny will be revealed. You will see the path before you more clearly and your powers will reveal themselves quite dramatically. That's what began to happen on Yagdi when you both came to my defense."

Whitney began to look apprehensive once again, so Ursula reminded her, "Don't forget, you have a powerful ally in your necklace. Its three stones were specifically chosen to assist you as we move forward." Some of her confidence was returning, but she still wondered how Ursula planned to proceed and asked, "How can you possibly make something feel the least bit threatening while we're standing in my bright cheerful kitchen?"

Impressed that the girl's eagerness to begin was tempered with the reality of what she was seeing in front of her, Ursula answered, "That's a very good question, young Whitney. How indeed can we accomplish that?" With a confident smile, she explained, "First and foremost, always trust your instincts. You've yet to realize how strong yours are, but they've been serving you well for these past thirteen years. At the same time, don't always listen to what your eyes show you or your ears whisper to you. Your Earthly senses can be unintentionally deceiving and therefore get in the way. There's also the possibility of others manipulating your senses, like what you see or hear, to their advantage."

Taking a deep breath, Ursula was ready to begin. "We must pull those amazing powers out of you, young Whitney. To do so, I fear I must take extreme measures. I apologize in advance for what I must now do." With no warning, Ursula became a mist creature. Standing right in front of her, its horrid red eyes were full of hatred and both fisted claws were raised menacingly toward her. Even more terrifying, those horrid tentacles were beginning to appear on top of her head. As soon as they emerged, they began to writhe back and forth, darting in and out, as they stretched closer and closer to her.

She'd been terrorized by these creatures for a month now, and having one so close, she instinctively feared for her life. Ursula had advised her to trust those instincts. Concentrating on the apparition before her, Whitney raised both hands and placed them on her shoulders then shoved them toward the creature. Surprise shone in those hideous red eyes as its ugly squat body wabbled back and forth but righted itself quickly and began racing toward her.

Without much time to think, Whitney knew she had to do something fast. She put her hands up to her shoulders once again and pushed them outward with every ounce of energy and determination she could gather from within. This time she felt something she'd never felt before. An unfamiliar but strong force moved through her arms and into her hands as she pushed them toward the creature. Surprising her, the horrid creature actually fell over and crashed to the floor.

Rallying quickly, it shook its head, stood up and raced forward with increased urgency. The claws on its hands were spread out menacingly and the tentacles grew longer as they tried to reach her. Unexpectedly, the horrid creature changed direction and charged right toward poor little Aiden.

Whitney felt something erupt from deep inside, flooding her with confidence and removing any lingering doubts. She realized this creature threatening her little dragon was no match for her. Armed with that knowledge and intense rage, Whitney felt the same strange energy move into her arms. Yelling, "NO!" she shoved her hands toward the creature. This time, it was powerful enough to make the red-eyed enemy fly across the floor hitting the door with such force it crumpled to the ground and lay there motionless.

Shocked at her accomplishment, she hugged Aiden close. Not certain what would happen next, she remained vigilant and prepared in case it came at them again. The crumpled creature didn't awaken to attack them. Instead, the ugly body shimmered brilliantly then morphed back into Ursula's familiar shape.

Whitney felt awful and ran to help her up. Ursula was grinning from ear to ear as she rubbed her right hip. Looking proudly at her young warrior, Ursula crowed, "Whitney, never feel bad when you're forced to defend yourself or those you love! On Yagdi, that move is known as a 'Purmot,' which you mastered instinctively and with remarkable skill on your third attempt. I knew you had powers that we just needed to uncover. Did you notice your purmot became stronger when you were forced to defend Aiden rather than yourself? Let's do it again!" Several challenges later, Whitney felt increasingly confident and had learned to call on her new-found power with reassuring consistency.

With no warning, Ursula became an ugly troll-like creature with warts all over its head. It walked on two legs but used its arms to help balance its movement. Whitney thought it looked a lot like the huge jungle gorillas she'd learned about on TV. Remembering how intelligent those gorillas can be, she feared the same might be true of this unexpected creature.

Moving more quickly than she'd expected, the troll lunged at a poor unsuspecting Aiden who instantly curled into a little ball cowering in fear.

Ms. Ellie had had enough of this awful game at the little dragon's expense, so she joined Whitney in defending the little guy. Transforming into her true form as a majestic panther, she prepared to pounce on their enemy. At the same time, Whitney purmotted. This time, she did so with such force it not only knocked the creature down but tossed it across the kitchen. Flying through the air, the huge troll-like thing crashed into the stove, leaving a huge dent where it hit.

The panther's yellow eyes were full of admiration as she watched Whitney effectively take out their enemy. Satisfied the threat had been removed, she returned to cat form, and ran up to sniff Aiden's nose sympathetically then began to purr, trying her best to comfort the little dragon.

Whitney ran to poor Ursula who was sitting upright with her back against the stove, looking a bit dazed. Grinning up at her young protégé, she announced in a weakened voice, "You pack a powerful punch, young Whitney. Will you help me up once again dear? Time is of the essence and we must forge ahead."

Shaking her head, Whitney helped her friend stand up, but this time she guided her to the table and helped her sit down. "I don't care about your 'time is of the essence,' Ursula. You need to sit and rest for a minute. I'll get you some water," and raced over to the sink.

Bringing the water to Ursula, she sat down across from her. "This is too rough on you. I don't want to knock you over anymore. Can we do something else?"

Grinning with excitement, Ursula smiled and pronounced, "Your true colors certainly shine when someone you love is in trouble, don't they? Bravo! We certainly can!"

• • •

In the meantime, Edward stood on the beach staring inquisitively at Mergan, becoming increasingly impatient to begin. Finally, the wizard announced, "Edward, I've determined how best to help you discover your talents, so how about we get right to it?"

Edward began to jump in place with nervous energy as the wizard continued, "I will be here as your guide, so I'll only offer assistance if it's absolutely necessary. Never forget you have a formidable ally in that Merlinite stone you're wearing."

Tired of all the talk with no action, Edward looked up and gasped. Hundreds of hideous creatures were flying toward them with supernatural speed. Approaching from all directions, there were so many their iridescent purple bodies almost completely blocked the blue sky. Edward knew they'd be on them in seconds, so he threw his hand high over his head, then separated his arms in an arc-like motion back toward the ground, just as he'd done on Yagdi. There, it had created some kind of short-lived barrier. This time, he was dismayed when the strange birds hit nothing and continued flying right toward them.

Out of nowhere, a thought occurred. Following his instincts, he raised one hand high over his head, and spread his fingers wide then rotated it slowly toward the ground in a big sweeping arc. At the same time, he touched his Merlinite stone with the other hand. A few of the flying monstrosities appeared to smash into something then simply disappeared. That was satisfying, however, not completely successful. Most of them flew right through his 'invisible dome' and swooped down to peck his head then dart quickly away. Hovering menacingly, they returned for more pecks, again and again.

Those birds were becoming a pain in the neck, literally. It took a lot of concentration and he had to work fast to fend off most of the nasty flying beasts. Concerned for the wizard, Edward took his eyes off the birds for a quick glance toward the mage. Mergan was laughing so hard he had to hold his stomach.

In extreme irritation, Edward looked toward the flying creatures once again. The sight of them still filled him with dread, however anger fueled his next move. He was so upset with the wizard for laughing at him, he held both his arm up with renewed energy. Rather than his sweeping arc toward the ground, he moved both hands toward his merry coach with a great deal of force. What happened next surprised him. The movement hadn't stopped the birds but had succeeded in rerouting them. Their small hideous bodies flew away from him and right toward the unsuspecting mage.

Mergan's laughter turned to surprised disbelief at the youngster's audacity. Recovering quickly, he nonchalantly raised his staff, as if he had all the time in the world, and the entire flock of creatures simply disappeared. "I really need one of those!" Edward mumbled.

Bringing his stick back down to the ground, Mergan looked at Edward and smiled then started clapping. His smile looked quite forced and more like a straight line, and his bushy brows were still furrowed while he clapped, but Edward knew his trainer approved.

Scratching his head where he'd gotten pecked by those nasty birds, Edward strode purposefully toward the mage. Expecting to hit the useless barrier he'd tried to create, he held his hands in front of him, but made it to Mergan unencumbered. With a combination of anger and curiosity, he spit out, "What was that all about?"

Very pleased, Mergan explained, "Splendid, young Edward! You actually harnessed the wind and used it to propel your enemy away. Toward me, I might add. Just for your information, that ability is called Purrmotting. To catch me by surprise is quite rare indeed. We've just discovered a very rare and powerful gift that will be extremely helpful if you're forced to protect yourself, Whitney and little Aiden."

Edward was still staring at him, waiting to hear more, so he coughed and took a sip of water from his bottle then continued. "When you first saw the birds, you understandably felt threatened. You reacted to that threat by using a talent known on Yagdi as Wafting. When you felt threatened, you were able to create a protective dome around yourself. It didn't work as well as you'd hoped, but I promise you it soon will."

"I might add, you were at your best, and quite creative, when you became angry with me." Looking quite pleased, the mage continued, "We need to practice that a few more times, then see if you can protect Whitney and little Aiden inside your dome."

Just then, snakes began slithering toward them from the

dunes. At the same time, huge unnatural waves rose out of the otherwise calm lake and raced toward them, growing larger and more threatening as they approached.

Trying to Waft, Edward put one hand into the air and splayed his fingers wide, while holding his Merlinite with the other. This time, he created enough of an invisible shield to block both the snakes and waves. Thousands of nasty snakes hit the invisible shield and disappeared, just like the flying creatures. However, Edward was intrigued when the waves didn't disappear as they smashed against his barrier. They simply calmed to become mere ripples then raced back down the beach and into the water. Watching the receding waves, Edward asked, "Why didn't the waves disappear like the ravens and snakes?"

Mergan loved to teach but enjoyed being listened to even more. Therefore, using his knowledge of things both natural and unnatural, he began a long, drawn-out answer. "Natural elements, like the water in Earth's Great Lakes, react differently to spells. They have strong forces of their own and are capable of removing any spells cast on them. That's a wonderful piece of knowledge to tuck away for a rainy day."

Leading Edward toward the house, Mergan said, "You've done well for your first lesson, young Edward. Let's find our two allies and relax after a day well spent learning new skills. That's always exhilarating, isn't it?"

Noticing the time on the kitchen clock, Edward was dismayed that it was later than he'd thought. Wanting to get some training time in before heading home, he drank the cocoa Ursula handed him, then prepared to say good-bye.

However, before he rushed off, Ursula jumped up and clapped her hands to announce, "Today went so well, and we all learned a lot. It was exciting, was it not? Tomorrow will be even more fun! Just be prepared for some thrilling new challenges!"

With that intriguing thought, Edward went out the back door

and down the flight of stairs to the beach where he'd parked his bike. Waving, he headed toward the campground, unable to stop himself from looking up occasionally to see if any nasty birds were following him.

# Chapter Twenty

# A NEW DEVELOPMENT

Day two of their training started way too early. Ursula woke before dawn to prepare another one of her 'specialty breakfasts' of pancakes and eggs, with Aiden and Ms. Ellie eagerly assisting. When breakfast was ready, she went to the stairs and announced loudly, "Breakfast is served. Come quickly while it's still warm!"

Mergan and Whitney entered the kitchen looking rather disheveled, a bit grumpy and far from hungry. To their dismay, there was no time to wake up slowly, because their chef was wide awake and eager to get the day started. Finding seats at the table, they sleepily watched her bring volumes of food to the table, while she sang some happy tune.

Knowing her grumpy old friend needed coffee above all else, Ursula brought a steaming cup loaded with sugar to Mergan and hoped it would improve his mood. Not looking at her, he simply wrapped his hands around the much-needed mug of caffeine and grunted a low guttural 'thanks.'

Bringing a glass of orange juice to Whitney, Ursula was just sitting down across from her when Edward came through the back door looking as tired as Whitney felt. Dropping into an empty chair, he yawned and admitted he wasn't very hungry. At that, Ursula clucked her tongue and wiggled a finger at him. "You two have a lot to learn today, and food not only feeds the stomach but your mind as well. Eat young man!"

Hearing her admonishment of Edward's lack of appetite, Whitney kept hers to herself and poked around at her food while Ursula talked. Her lighthearted demeanor gone, she seriously discussed the week ahead, and reemphasized time was of the essence.

"Mergan and I stayed up well into the night discussing yesterday's successes. We're pretty confident we've come up with the perfect outline of activities and challenges for the remainder of the week." Wanting to share their plan with the two trainees she began to explain. "We uncovered very special gifts in each of you yesterday. You both purmotted to harness the winds, and Edward created a protective dome using a talent known as wafting. Today, we must put both skills to good use, and practice them using more threatening scenarios."

Whitney thought that sounded rather ominous. However, the caffeine had apparently worked its magic on Mergan because he jumped in with excitement in his voice. "Your gifts were revealed even sooner than we'd hoped, young ones. I'm especially pleased with how quickly you learned to use them." Whitney saw Ursula beam at his praises and wondered if she considered them directed at her as well.

If that hadn't been Mergan's intent, Whitney thought it should have been. Ursula had been the one to find her and Edward. Then, she'd gently encouraged them to accept all the strange new developments that threatened to change their lives forever. Deep in thought, she'd only been half listening to Mergan, that is until his unexpected and disturbing announcement.

Looking apologetically to his student and friend, he shocked them all by saying, "I'm afraid I must ask Ursula to leave you sooner than we'd planned. Our enemy's skirmishes have increased in frequency and are becoming more threatening to the good creatures on Yagdi. Therefore, as much as I know she'd like to stay here with you, she really must return home. Her wise insights and talents are sorely needed!"

Whitney noticed Ursula's surprise at her mentor's announcement, as well as the moment sadness crept in, threatening to overwhelm her poor friend. Normally full of positive energy, Whitney watched Ursula put down her fork and sigh. Then, not making eye contact with any of them, she focused on her uneaten plate of food.

Whitney grew angry at the Wizard and his poor communication skills. She wished she could wave a magic wand and turn back time to her friend's carefree preparation of their breakfast. Moments later, Ursula squared her shoulders and looked directly at Mergan. "I knew my time here would be brief, but I truly thought I had more of it. However, Mergan is always correct in his assessments. Because I must leave sooner rather than later, we must work even harder and with greater speed."

Ursula saw Whitney's eyes tear up. Not wanting to show her own distress, she looked away. Then, with a little sniffle, she coughed and explained, "You are both critical to our success because you'll be guarding our precious young Aiden. Your protection will give him the time he needs to grow into adulthood safely. He will actually grow surprisingly fast. In less than two months, he will be old enough, and big enough, to claim his rightful place as the mighty ruler of our world. Torryn is growing quite old and eagerly awaits the day he can transfer the crown to his son. What a time for celebration that will be, and of course, you both must join us. Everyone will want to honor you for keeping our young king safe!"

Startled at how quickly young Aiden would mature, Whitney grew even sadder. She hadn't realized she'd be saying good-bye to all of her friends so soon. Ursula saw the young girl's sadness was increasing and jumped in sympathetically, "This is very difficult on all of us. I wish things were different. One day in the future, I hope we'll be able to enjoy each other's company without the threat of enemies at our door. However, for you to be prepared, it is important that you know what lies ahead."

Returning to the topic of their little dragon, she continued, "Dragons grow extremely quickly, so in the next few weeks, our little dragon will triple in size and by the end of August he should be fully grown."

Realizing she had concerned poor Whitney and confused young Edward, Ursula continued, "However, don't forget that dragons are quite capable of 'fitting into their environment.' Aiden will stay relatively small while in the confines of your home, Whitney. To others, like your mother, he'll simply grow to look like a year-old puppy, so neither of you has to worry about his size becoming an issue."

Looking at the two young chosen ones, she finished by admitting, "You both have an extremely important challenge while Aiden is growing to adulthood under your protection. Our little future king must literally learn to spread his wings while he grows into his magnificent grandeur. That must happen secretly in a very private location. That's so critical, I suggest that you learn a convenient spell designed to remove memories, just in case someone happens to witness one of your training sessions."

Looking at Mergan, she winked and suggested, "We have just the man to take care of that little problem. Mergan is loaded with useful little spells, so I'm certain he can come up with something. Am I correct in that assumption, Mage?"

Looking from the kids to his former student, Mergan considered her question carefully for a few moments, then pounded his stick on the floor saying, "My staff and I have just the spell for a situation such as that." His positive attitude brought a huge smile to Ursula's wrinkled face and her hands clapped in delight as her good humor returned. At the same time, Edward thought, "So that's what his stick is called. I've got to ask Mergan how I can get my hands on one and learn to use it!"

Looking at the two young chosen ones, Ursula repeated, "You have both been well chosen for this task, and I know this week will be enlightening, challenging and full of surprises, so how about we finish breakfast and get started?"

Whitney noticed the gleam in Mergan's eyes and wondered what they had up their sleeves. Looking sympathetically toward Edward, she noticed he was looking at them with an equal amount of curiosity and unease.

The rest of breakfast was spent in light conversation, providing some necessary wake-up time for everyone except Ursula. She always seemed wide awake and excited to meet whatever challenges came her way. Looking sadly at her new friend, Whitney could see why she would be missed by her friends and allies on Yagdi and it made sense she had to return. Her boundless energy and enthusiasm alone would be a necessary infusion of hope if things were spinning out of control.

As breakfast ended, Whitney said out loud, "I hope you can find a way to rid Yagdi of such a horrid enemy once and for all. Edward and I will work very hard to prove to you both that we're ready to protect little Aiden before you have to leave us."

Looking fondly at the little dragon, Whitney continued, "So, I promise to work as hard as I can to learn what needs to be learned and earn that trust from you both."

With tears threatening to flood out of her already moistened eyes, Ursula rushed to Whitney and gave her one of her huge bear hugs. "Oh, my dear girl, you already have. We just need to polish things up a bit." Then with a grin, she turned toward Edward, "And what do you say, young Edward? Are you in as well?"

Edward's grin was so huge it forced that rare dimple to appear and he vehemently announced, "I was in as soon as I learned I could shove those nasty birds toward Mergan yesterday. The shock on his face was worth all the pecks I got learning how to perfect it." Noticing the scowl on Mergan's face, accompanied by a hint of laughter in his eyes, he continued, "I can't wait to try it on my sister!"

Seeing their horrified faces, he knew his joke hadn't gone over very well, so he quickly explained, "Just kidding, geez! But seriously, this discussion today confirmed it. Yes, I promise to work hard and earn your trust before you head back to Yagdi. I want you to prepare for battle without worrying about little Aiden, or either of us for that matter."

The Mage stood up and once again pounded his staff on the floor, making everyone look at him. Clearing his throat, he proceeded in a voice filled with admiration for their young chosen ones. "Thank you both for your concern over our well-being. I admit we face troubling times in our world, and our enemy has become quite strong, but they're not yet invincible. It is time to develop a course of action and we must plan to strike offensively as soon as possible. However, with that in mind, it's equally important that we have a smooth transition of power from father to son."

Looking at Whitney and Edward, he continued, "Keeping Aiden safe might very well become quite dangerous. I know that our enemies are looking for him as we speak. They know his capture would seal our fate and allow them to seize the power they so desperately crave. Thank you for risking your lives to keep our future king safe from harm."

The wizard looked toward Ursula for approval and at her subtle nod, continued. "If things go terribly wrong and we begin to lose the battle, we will send for both of you, Ms. Ellie and little Aiden. Trust that we will only do so as a last resort, hoping the unexpected arrival of the future King of Yagdi will instill fear in our enemies and cause chaos. Assuming that we're correct, we have a back-up plan in place for a crushing offensive blow while their army is in disarray."

The mage surprised Whitney and Edward by admitting, "You must now see how important it is you both remain safe, so you're able to keep Aiden protected and hidden from the eyes of our enemies. We need to win this war to ensure the heart and soul of Yagdi lives on." He stopped to direct his piercing gaze at Edward and Whitney then continued, "Our success depends on all of us sitting at this table. Ursula and I have discussed this and realize if you must become involved, we should develop a plan together, and use your expertise."

# Chapter Twenty-One

# A UNIFIED PLAN

The dumfounded look on their young faces, was proof to Ursula they were feeling terribly overwhelmed. However, she knew this important discussion must continue to its completion. Whitney and Edward needed to know just how crucial their role as Aiden's protectors would become if they needed to reenter her portal and return to Yagdi.

Thinking it best to begin with something Whitney could help with, she asked, "It's critical that we find a place appropriately isolated for little Aiden's training. Whitney, you know this area quite well. Do you have any ideas?"

Considering all the alternatives, Whitney's first idea was Ellie's Point, but if Aiden was flying it was too open to inquisitive eyes. Then she had a brilliant idea and suggested with excitement, "Ursula, at our BBQ, you told Edward's grandparents there was a house for rent in town. Can you magically 'arrange' for them to decide to take that house and store their camper at the forest service campground for the winter?"

Instantly grasping Whitney's idea, Ursula eagerly nodded her head, promising she would find a way to coerce Edward's grandparents into renting the house in town, while thinking it was their decision. She would also arrange for the National Forest Service Director to allow them to store their camper in the campground while they moved into town.

Growing more excited with her plan, Whitney explained, "The forest service always lowers a thick steel gate across the entrance to the campground when the season ends. That's usually the Tuesday after Labor Day weekend. However, this year they're closing a whole month earlier because of the beetle infestation. They want to spray pesticides early enough to provide the time necessary to kill the increasing population of pests before the first frost, and they can't do that while people are still camping. Once that steel gate is in place and locked, it makes an effective barricade for most vehicles. If we added a few downed trees on either side of the entrance, we would eliminate any chance of someone ignoring the gate and attempting to drive around it to get back to the campground."

Thinking of all possible intrusions, she added, "The possibility of a stray hiker wandering into the area is remote but could happen. You said you could teach us how to erase problematic memories. Doing that would ensure no one remembers seeing our practice sessions, even if they found their way to the camper. My vote would be to use that trailer as our training site."

Edward agreed with Whitney, which forced him to consider another possibility. "I'll need to stay longer, won't I? Can you arrange for that to happen, Ursula?" At her enthusiastic nod, he continued, "I can stay with my grandparents in town, and make sure they give me a key to their camper. I'll explain that I need to use the key to periodically check on it to make sure the colder temperatures aren't affecting their summer home. I'll make one for Whitney too."

Suddenly, Edward had a great idea he thought was worth sharing. "If we become threatened by your enemies, and help can't arrive immediately, my grandparents' camper tucked away in the woods would be a perfect spot to hide until you or someone you trust can bring us to Yagdi or send word we need to enter the portal."

All four lapsed into thoughtful silence. Ursula and Mergan looked quite pleased with the creative ideas from both Whitney and Edward and looked at each other with relief and increasing admiration for their young trainees.

Nodding enthusiastically, Ursula added, "We have a plan to give you advance warning when things are becoming dire on Yagdi and that we'll soon be needing your assistance. Its success depends on your stones, however, so you must promise to always wear them from now on." Taking a moment to look intently at each of them, she repeated, "I can't stress enough how crucial it is to our plan that you always have your stones on!"

In a very serious tone, she continued, "Your safety may become compromised if our common enemy gains the upper hand in battle. You'll know things are going poorly for us because your nightmares will return as our enemies once again try to enter your world or draw you into ours. That concern prompted us to develop new plans for you both after we leave Earth. Thanks to Mergan's expertise in unusual phenomenon, he was able to cast an additional spell on your stones. They will continue to become hot if danger is approaching. However, if that danger has become dire enough that Mergan or I must send a warning to you, your stones will now become ice cold. That will only happen if your location has been discovered by our enemies and they're headed your way. Unfortunately, due to the distance between our worlds, the warning may only provide you with minutes to react. Therefore, you must promise us you will heed that warning immediately, grab Aiden and Ms. Ellie and race for the camper in the forest without delay."

Ursula saw Whitney's concerned expression, and knew it wasn't concern for herself, but for her mother. Not at all surprised, and respecting her love and loyalty, especially when it came to her mom, Ursula reminded her, "They aren't after your mother, young Whitney. As soon as you leave, you save Susan because they will follow you and leave her in peace. We will also create some kind of diversion designed to ease your mother's concern over your sudden absence. Leave that to Mergan and me. As soon as we've come up with an idea that's rock solid, we'll share it with you. Can you live with that, young Whitney?"

Ursula was relieved when the look in Whitney's eyes turned from concerned to fiercely determined. Filled with admiration, she admitted, "Your concern for others at least equals that for yourself. I know you'll do whatever it takes to keep your mother safe, so I have no doubt you will leave in haste if the stones warn you to do so."

Turning toward young Edward, Ursula repeated her reassurances that his grandparents should remain unharmed once he left. The same relief appeared on his strong determined face, prompting Ursula to admit, "The two of you are quite amazing and I have developed a lasting fondness for both of you. Mergan and I are grateful that, in spite of the innocence and naivety of youth, you both understand the importance of winning this war and have promised to help all the good and decent creatures of our land. You have an extremely strong motivator if you must battle enemies to keep each other safe, and that is the strong bond that now exists between all of you. We will leave Earth knowing you're well equipped and highly motivated, and that gives us great relief."

Not wanting to reveal the strong emotions threatening to break through his intentionally gruff exterior, Mergan coughed, took another sip of coffee, and announced, "I agree with Ursula one hundred percent. You are both impressive and such a pleasure to work with. I have come to realize that your desire to learn matches that of Ursula's and my own. Thank you from the bottom of my heart for your strong desire to help us! However, I believe we've discussed enough for today. It's time for some active learning, don't you think?" Seeing the excitement in their eyes, he explained, "We will continue what we began yesterday with renewed vigor. Failure is not an option for any of us. We must focus on learning from each other while we're still together."

Feeling energized by their mage's surprising gratitude, Whitney and Edward were eager to continue their lessons. They would be on their own if and when their enemies arrived, so their lives and the lives of their two friends depended on their accomplishments this week.

Edward admitted this was far bigger than even his upcoming triathlon. He'd still train for that, and participate, but he now had something far more important to prepare for. He knew his stubborn determination would rise to this challenge. Sneaking a glance at Whitney, her fierce expression made him very proud. They would be a strong and highly motivated team.

Whitney stared at the group around her and announced abruptly, "What are we waiting for? Let's do this!" and moved toward the door. Opening it, she looked back impatiently for everyone to join her, which they promptly did.

Little Aiden didn't know why they were all so excited, but he joined in, running in circles and leaping on everyone. He wanted to be a part of whatever fun activity he sensed was about to happen. "Let the games begin!" Whitney yelled as they all headed toward the beach.

Whitney's level of energy was so high she was practically bouncing up and down on the beach waiting for the first set of instructions. Edward's apparent calm was in direct contrast, but his eyes showed a grim resolve.

Watching Aiden and Ellie race down the beach with enthusiastic energy, Ursula turned to Whitney and Edward and said, "It looks like you'll have to work hard to keep up with that level of energy, so let's get started. Yesterday, we discovered some of your gifts, but I'm certain there are more to unveil."

Knowing how eager they were to train, Ursula still had some

assessments to complete before that began, so she explained, "There are certain traits I've noticed in each of you that are indicators of hidden talents. Whitney you have a high level of sensitivity toward others' feelings and emotions, and I've seen you use what we call a 'sixth sense,' or premonition, when you have strong feelings things aren't quite right but are still beyond your understanding. I'd like to create some scenarios to assess the strength of those two traits.

Looking at Edward she continued, "You are already quite strong physically, and have a high level of confidence in your ability to compete among your peers. Your willingness to work hard and do whatever it takes to win might be useful in countering threatening behavior from those seeking to harm you or those you must protect. In other words, you don't accept defeat easily, and that could be a very strong weapon if we can find a way to perfect it."

Continuing to think out loud as she sorted through possibilities, Ursula suggested, "Your physical abilities were impressive when you were confronted with imminent threats. You reacted quite naturally and I'm certain you could repeat that over and over again without much difficulty. What we need to work on today is sensing the existence of threats before they actually appear."

While speaking, Ursula's mind began formulating a plan for the two to work on as a team. "Whitney, we must confirm whether you have the ability to anticipate the arrival of an enemy, because that would give you quite an edge. That gives us a worthy training goal for today. We can fine tune that ability as needed. That, combined with Edward's physical strength and determination to win at all costs, would create a very formidable team. Therefore, I believe we should work on training as a team today so we can determine if your individual talents can be merged. If Whitney can truly anticipate the arrival of danger, our goal will become apparent. We would learn to first use Whitney's ability to anticipate trouble. However, that needs to be coordinated with Edward's physical strength and determination to win if you must battle the enemy. Does that make sense to everyone?"

Watching Ursula with the young ones, Mergan was proud of how well he'd trained his former student. When she'd first arrived for his tutelage so many years ago, his initial assessments showed she was extraordinary and destined for greatness. Although thrilled at the opportunity to mentor such talent, he knew it would challenge even his immense abilities to create inspiring lessons.

Ursula's physical abilities, such as changing her appearance and harnessing the wind for travel, were remarkable, however he had chosen to focus more on her keen mind. She had a natural ability to accurately assess any situation then determine the most effective course of action. He'd decided to perfect those talents because he knew they would benefit the citizens of their world the most when they became necessary.

His prize student had been so invigorated by his challenging lessons, she had relished hard work and thus became the best strategist in their world. Those skills, when paired with her warmth and deep concern for others, made her such an outstanding general. Her presence was sorely missed as Yagdi's protectors who worked under her direction finalized their battle plans.

Their Dragon King was acting as temporary general until she returned. Although sharing many of her qualities, the wise dragon admitted everything worked more smoothly when Ursula was present.

With all those thoughts racing through his mind, and knowing they needed to return to Yagdi without much more delay, Mergan decided on a plan to move forward. Planting his staff firmly into the sand, he was gratified to see their attention immediately focused on him. "Whitney and Edward," he announced, "I want you to sit down in the sand and try to block everything out. Close your eyes and breathe deeply. Listen to the sound of the gentle waves on the shore and feel the sun's warmth on your faces."

Listening to Mergan's quiet voice, Whitney felt herself relax as she enjoyed the peaceful sound of the waves, and eventually stopped listening to him completely. Suddenly, she felt a throbbing on the top of her head, as if she were getting a headache. The throbbing moved down the back of her head and into her shoulders, making them extremely tense, almost to the point of aching. Wondering about the abrupt physical change, she looked toward Edward to see if he was bothered too, but he looked completely calm and still had his eyes closed.

On full alert now, Whitney felt goosebumps and thought, "This is strange. I've never experienced anything like this before." She sensed something was going on, but it was very subtle. Suddenly, everything around her grew blurry and distorted, as if she was looking through a very old window with thick, uneven glass.

Feeling their presence before seeing them, Whitney frantically turned to look in all directions. There, still too far away to identify, she saw a large black cloud of something approaching with unnatural speed. Jumping up, she yelled to Edward, "Something's approaching really fast, but I can't tell what it is. Find Aiden and Ellie and bring them here now!"

Edward saw them a little way down the beach romping in the waves. Not wasting any time, he ran to them as if all of their lives depended on his speed. Picking them up, he ran back to Whitney, noticing their weight didn't slow him down the slightest.

While Edward was racing down the beach, Whitney motioned for Ursula and Mergan to look up, ensuring they were aware of the approaching danger. She knew they could fend for themselves, so she focused on the three returning to her.

Edward looked in the direction Whitney pointed and was dismayed to see the horrid birds he'd just dealt with the day before.

Knowing what he must do, he placed Aiden and Ellie on the ground then put one hand in the air with fingers outstretched while the other wrapped around his stone. As soon as he touched the stone, he successfully wafted, creating a large dome over all four of them. Whitney hoped Edward knew what he was doing because she was busy sheltering Aiden. Ms. Ellie was standing close to them, ready to shape shift into a panther if need be.

Just as Whitney had predicted, the menacing birds were on them in no time, but Edward's protective dome held true and the flying monsters disappeared as soon as they hit his shield. This time, not one of them snuck through. Sighing with relief, they high-fived each other and picked up Ellie and Aiden to hug them close.

Once the threat had been eliminated, the pounding in Whitney's head disappeared, along with the tenseness in her shoulders and goosebumps. Looking over at Ursula and Mergan, she was relieved to see they no longer looked blurry but quite normal once again. Their behavior wasn't quite normal, however, because both had begun to clap and dance around Mergan's staff.

Grinning, Whitney and Edward put the excited and wriggling dragon and cat down so they could race off to romp with the two elders. The dome was no longer there to prohibit them moving about the beach, so they'd discovered something else important. Apparently, Edward's dome shield only lasted as long as there was a threat. As they watched the celebration, Whitney and Edward looked at each other with satisfaction, knowing something major had just been accomplished.

# Chapter Twenty-Two

# WHAT'S NEXT?

They all walked up to the deck feeling like a huge burden had been removed. Mergan was really smiling now, a true smile; and Ursula's walk looked more like a merry dance. The little dragon and cat were definitely enjoying the celebratory mood and chased each other in circles as they raced up the steep stairs.

Once settled in comfortable chairs, they sipped Whitney's fresh-squeezed lemonade, and gazed contentedly over the lake. Ursula was not one to remain silent for too long, so she broke the silence by complimenting her two young friends. "You were the very best out there, young ones!" You rose to the challenge extremely well and proved my hypotheses beyond a shadow of a doubt. Whitney, you can indeed predict the arrival of danger and Edward you're well equipped to move fast, use your strength and shield all four of you. Congratulations on a job well done. You've just eased our minds and made our hearts lighter when we must leave you."

Smiling at Whitney she suggested, "You, my dear, must have some sessions with Mergan to learn how to enhance your awareness of subtle disturbances without his assistance. Our mage just helped you relax, which allowed your mind to sense the presence of things beyond your sight, and then warn you. That's the ability that I thought I'd detected in you. Not only could you sense the disturbance before it became visible, but you took charge with ease and confidence."

"And Edward, you instinctively chose to believe Whitney and follow her direction, even though you hadn't sensed anything was amiss yourself. You were able to enhance your natural abilities when the urgency of the situation demanded it. I'll bet you didn't feel the weight of either Aiden or Ms. Ellie when you picked them up to run back to Whitney. "Am I correct?" When Edward nodded, she explained, "That's what I mean by enhanced natural abilities. That is exactly what needs to happen and your reaction to Whitney's advance warning was perfect. You are in fact the formidable team we'd hoped to discover today and couldn't ask for more. We're quite pleased, are we not, Mergan?"

Nodding, Mergan said, "I must admit for your first team challenge, you were quite remarkable." With a gleam in his eye, he continued, "Whitney, I agree that you and I should spend some practice time together to fine tune your ability to tune into things that may be out of sight but can be exposed with expert guidance." Seeing all of them grin at his playful arrogance, he smiled and said, "It looks like our challenges must become more difficult as the week progresses!"

Praises and confidence in their abilities had Whitney and Edward both looking pleased. They knew this had been a test and they'd just passed with flying colors.

Whitney asked, "How do I know when I need to relax my mind so I can tune into things around me?"

Mergan thought that was an outstanding question and answered, "Once you've successfully completed all of my strategically chosen lessons, your mind will automatically tune into things beyond your existing senses. At that point, you won't have to do a thing. However, you must also learn how to assess whether that hidden presence is dangerous and, if so, the level of danger."

Noticing the look of worry on Whitney's face he smiled and shared calmly, "You don't have to worry about being constantly bombarded with useless information. It doesn't happen like that.

Your mind is a remarkable thing, and you're simply going to learn to use it more effectively."

To ease her uncertainty, Mergan explained, "Our training sessions will focus on teaching your mind what you consider to be life threatening. Through practice sessions, we will teach your mind to recognize only those threats then relay that information to you. Your brain will analyze things so quickly and efficiently, you won't even know anything's amiss until it nudges you as it did today. You'll experience the same symptoms you had on the beach. Does that make sense, Whitney?"

Considering what he'd just divulged, Whitney finally nodded with a proud grin. "I'm amazing, aren't I?"

Very seriously, Mergan nodded and agreed, "You are amazing indeed, young Whitney."

Edward had been watching and listening carefully. When Whitney and Mergan were finished, he looked at Mergan and asked, "Can you train me to do that too?"

Taken off guard by the young man's surprising request, Mergan looked at Ursula. Seeing the subtle shake of her head, he said, "I'm sorry, Edward, but that isn't one of your gifts. However, it's quite apparent you can harness incredible strength and speed when it's necessary. Even though it comes so naturally to you, we'll continue to perfect it throughout what's left of this week."

Noticing his disappointment, the wizard reminded Edward, "You both have gifts that are quite remarkable, however you are most powerful when you combine your talents and work together. You are both stubborn and competitive, which are usually wonderful traits if working alone. In your case, however, they're balanced nicely by your overwhelming desire to do whatever it takes to keep each other safe. That's what I find the most remarkable and satisfying!"

Mergan and Ursula looked at each other, then back at Edward, sensing he had something else troubling him. Prompting him,

Ursula asked, "Do you have something else to clear up, young man?"

Running his hand through his perpetually disheveled hair, Edward blurted, "I'm competing in a major triathlon in a few short weeks. Are these enhanced abilities going to give me an advantage? I'm trying to figure out if I should drop out. As much as I thrive on competition, and want to race, I don't want to do it unfairly."

Seeing the disappointment on his face, and admiring his desire to compete fairly, Whitney acknowledged there were all kinds of things to like about this particular biker boy. Trying to reassure him, she said, "Ursula and Mergan told us earlier your abilities are enhanced when lives are threatened. There's nothing life-threatening about a bike race, so maybe you'd simply be using your own abilities," then looked at her friend for confirmation.

Although she wanted to say how impressed she was with his need to compete fairly, Ursula deferred to her mage to address his concern. Grinning at Edward, he announced, "You just sealed my respect, young man. There are very few who wouldn't want to take advantage of enhanced abilities to 'win.' You, however, want to ensure you compete fairly. What a remarkable quality to own!"

Mergan quickly assured Edward that Whitney was in fact correct. "The enhanced abilities we witnessed on the beach will only emerge in life-threatening situations. How well you do in your upcoming triathlon, however, will be a result of your own natural abilities. You mustn't discount how much you've improved those natural abilities through your commendable commitment to hard training. I applaud your drive to work hard for things you want badly enough. Long story short, and I admit I am inclined to explain things to death, if you do well, you have none other than yourself to congratulate."

Edward appeared satisfied and quite relieved, but there was something else on Whitney's mind. "What happens if I sense danger is coming while I'm in my house with Aiden, but Edward's in town with his grandparents?"

Ursula broke in to answer. "That's an outstanding question too, and one we were planning on getting to later in the week." Looking at Mergan for his approval to continue, she admitted, "First and foremost, it seems that for the time being you are fairly safe from the intrusive probing by our enemy. There's a reason your nightmares haven't returned in recent days and will most certainly stay away for at least a short while longer."

"Our enemies have been distracted preparing for war, just as we are. As long as we can hold them at bay, and keep them busy with small skirmishes, they won't bother the two of you. However, as I explained earlier, if your nightmares return, that will be an important advance warning that we're losing the small skirmishes and they now have time to begin looking for young Aiden, and the two of you."

Looking at their concerned frowns, she continued, "It's important you hear the truth from us at all times, even if it's not great news. So, in all honesty, we fear we haven't figured out the logistics of the two of you being separated by distance yet. We're working on it, but we can share a plan we've discussed. It's not perfect, but it's straightforward and relatively easy. Mergan, would you like to be the one to explain?"

The mage nodded and continued where Ursula had left off, "We all agree Whitney will sense danger first, correct?" Seeing everyone nod, he continued, "If you sense danger, Whitney, it's critical you leave your house immediately and take Little Aiden and Ms. Ellie to the camper in the woods. However, you must both also remember that if danger is on your doorstep, you will receive that ice-cold warning from your stones."

Pausing to take another sip of lemonade, he continued, "Edward, when that happens, jump on that bike and ride as fast as you can to the campground. I'm certain your enhanced physical abilities will kick into high gear, because it'll be a life-or-death race, unlike any you've ever experienced. If our enemies have discovered the trailer, however, head immediately to the portal. We are the only two with the ability to enter Yagdi, so we came up with a plan for all of you to pass through if we can't be there. Be forewarned, however, once you enter, it's a one-way door. You won't be able to return to Earth without one of us accompanying you."

Seeing Whitney and Edward frown deeper, Ursula jumped in to explain, "It's a safeguard I put in place when I created the portal. I didn't want our enemies to discover they could travel between our worlds so easily using my portal."

Both Whitney and Edward had unknowingly leaned toward her as they listened with laser focused attention. In spite of their increased concern, Ursula wanted to keep them as safe as possible in her absence, so with eyes shining in sympathetic understanding, she proceeded.

"If events make it difficult or impossible for either Mergan or me to help you through the portal, Aiden will have the knowledge needed to assist you. The clues I placed in our little dragon when he was just a newborn will surface only if no other options remain."

The room had become eerily silent. Whitney noticed that even Ms. Ellie and Aiden were looking at Ursula in surprise, apparently understanding what she'd just revealed, and its importance. The little dragon cocked his head to the side, as if contemplating. Then, he grinned at Ursula and nodded, which made the scales on his head shimmer even more brightly.

Watching the little dragon carefully, Whitney was pretty certain she'd just seen him grow just a little in stature. She'd just witnessed the moment the little dragon became aware of his importance. She'd known all along that Aiden would soon learn of his destiny. However, she'd selfishly hoped it wouldn't be this soon, and realized she already missed the innocent little dragon she'd grown so fond of.

As if tuned into her emotions, Aiden leaped onto her lap and proceeded to energetically lick her face. Unable to stop herself, Whitney broke into a laugh which caused the little dragon to jump down and circle around and around chasing his tail in excitement. "I guess he's still a little guy after all," Whitney said.

A moment later, Mergan began to clap, slowly at first then faster and faster. Surprised at the wizard's unnatural exuberance, they looked expectantly toward him, awaiting an announcement of great importance. A man of few words, they were stunned to hear the wizard give Ursula one of his rare compliments. "Woman, you were born to take charge. You always think ahead with multiple outcomes in mind, prepared for any possible scenario. You amaze me!"

Ursula's shocked expression was immediately replaced with embarrassment as her face turned beet red from the unexpected but very welcome compliment. Smiling at his old friend, he attempted to take the attention off of her to give her time to recover.

Turning toward Whitney and Edward, he smiled and said in his booming voice, "I'd figured this discussion would produce many reactions in both of you. Bravo for turning your understandable confusion into determination. Minds become clearer once fear is cast aside!"

Whitney looked at the Wizard, then at Ursula, and was quite certain she spoke for both her and Edward when she admitted, "This is quite concerning and very scary. However, we know you will both do everything in your power to help us plan for all kinds of different possibilities. We trust your judgment, and know you'll be considering what's in our best interest, as well as young Aiden's." Looking at Edward, she said somewhat shyly, "I'm glad

Edward has my back too. I feel so much safer knowing I won't be alone."

Edward cleared his throat and nodded his agreement. "It's really overwhelming, and if your enemies do try to get to us it'll be frightening. However, I'm feeling more confident in my abilities today than I was yesterday. I know by the end of the week, my confidence and skills will grow even more, so I'm hoping my fears will lessen." Looking back at Whitney he admitted, "I've never depended on a girl to protect me, but I know you will and appreciate you having my back too, Whitney."

When they heard each one vow to protect the other, Ursula and Mergan smiled at each other. Mergan's voice cracked as he shared, "You are both well worth our time and effort and just as Ursula has said repeatedly, I too am very proud of you!"

Feeling a need to lighten the mood, Ursula jumped up to make sandwiches they all enjoyed on the deck then went back to the beach to continue their team practicing.

The rest of the week continued with no more huge revelations, but lots of practice time. Whitney learned to sense the presence of things only if they were a threat and they were able to ward off increasingly difficult adversaries. Their time together went by far too quickly, but they were all pleased with the results.

Whitney loved rising early each morning to tackle new challenges and thrived on the easy banter among very special friends. Therefore, as the end of the week drew near, she grew sadder and dreaded their quickly approaching last night together. To keep those emotions under control, she dove into her lessons with increased intensity.

Sure enough, that last night came all too soon. They were gathered at the dinner table enjoying a remarkably huge meal prepared by Ursula. Of course, it was pancakes and eggs once again, but this time she'd added bacon and hash browns. Whitney smiled at the spread, having decided days ago that Ursula either loved pancakes and eggs, or that was all she knew how to cook. But it didn't matter because it was a perfect way to enjoy each other's company.

As they were eating, they took turns talking about the week's successes and favorite memories. Before too long, they were all laughing at Edward getting pecked by the ravens on the first day. The sun had long since fallen below the horizon and the sky was darkening quickly. Wanting to get home before it was pitch dark, Edward stood up to say good-bye. Before he left, however, Whitney jumped up to say, "I'm turning thirteen on July 3rd, which is next Saturday. I hope all of you can come help me celebrate!"

Ursula had noticed Whitney's increasing sadness so readily agreed to the invitation saying, "That will be the perfect send-off for Mergan and myself and what a wonderful celebration it will be. Thank you for including us, young Whitney!"

Whitney felt tears bubble up at the thought of their departure, but held her head high and said, "My party will be more fun with all of you a part of it! By the way, are you going to break it to mom that Aiden will be staying with us, or is that up to me?"

Ursula grinned good naturedly and reassured Whitney she had it covered. Edward waved good-bye and went out the back door while Whitney and Mergan cleared the table of dirty dishes, washed them and put them all away. Ursula stayed seated and held Ms. Ellie. With a huge smile, she watched two very dear friends do all of the work, and realized she liked that a lot!

When they'd finished and sat for a short while enjoying each other's company, Mergan rose announcing he'd be sleeping else-where. Surprised at his decision to leave, Whitney asked, "You've slept here all week. Why are you leaving tonight?"

Mergan grinned and said, "It certainly isn't because I've grown weary of your company, young Whitney. However, your mother left a week ago saying farewell to her daughter and Ursula. I don't think she'd appreciate my joining the party without her prior approval. I respect that and want to alleviate any concern my presence might cause. Just as a word of caution, I think it best if your mom doesn't know what happened in her absence. The less she knows, the safer she'll remain."

Then he winked at her and added, "I promise to return for your party next Saturday, and I'm very much looking forward to it," then turned and walked out the door. Whitney ran to the door to wave good-bye, but the mage was no longer in sight. Shaking her head, she turned back to Ursula and said, "That man has more secrets than anyone can keep track of!"

Ursula laughed in agreement and admitted, "You're right, and that includes me, young Whitney! He's still full of mystery to me, even after so many years." Yawning, they said good night and headed toward their bedrooms.

Whitney didn't like the thought of this week coming to an end but was thrilled her mom would be home in less than twelve hours. Through all the week's excitement, she'd missed her and couldn't wait to have her back home!

Mergan's wise advice had once again put Whitney in the awkward position of keeping secrets from her mom, however she was becoming increasingly comfortable with it. Above all else, she wanted the most important person in her world to remain safe and would do whatever it took to ensure that outcome.

# Chapter Twenty-Three

## WHITNEY'S MOM RETURNS

Whitney and Ursula sat on the front porch under Susan's Veterinary sign, "Traveller's Rest," waiting for her mom's arrival. Whitney smiled thinking it was the perfect spot to welcome her home from the veterinary conference.

Whitney's leg was bouncing up and down excitedly and she was chewing on her thumbnail. Noticing her barely controlled excitement, Ursula smiled to herself as she watched the little dragon and cat chase each other through the trees playing hide-and-seek.

The plume of dust rising from the road announced Susan's arrival before they saw her car. Whitney ran out to the driveway and as soon as the car stopped and her mom opened the door, she pulled her out of her seat and into a huge bear hug.

Smiling back at her daughter and hugging her equally hard, she pushed Whitney out to arm's length to admire her beautiful daughter who would be a teenager in just one more week. Noticing how healthy and happy both her daughter and Ursula looked, Susan grinned, "What a greeting! Whitney, you look so good to me. I missed you so much! And look at your big smile. You look so happy!" then drew her daughter back in for another hug.

As if in silent agreement, both mother and daughter opened their arms to include Ursula in a group hug. Pulling her mother onto the porch to sit under her clinic sign, Whitney grinned and took orders for drinks then ran into the house for iced tea and lemonade.

As soon as her daughter was gone, Susan looked curiously at Ursula and asked half-seriously, "Okay, where did you hide my troubled daughter? I don't see any distress hiding behind her smile. All I see is happiness. Can you share your secret with me, Ursula?"

Smiling at Susan, Ursula only said, "We've been busy all week, and didn't have much time to mope around. She's been busy showing me a good time with lots of walks on the beach, and these two energetic youngsters have kept us moving. A friend of mine is in town and came to visit a few times. I hope you don't mind, but Whitney already asked him to her birthday party!"

Susan immediately agreed, "Of course your friend is welcome. The more the merrier!" Not wanting to pry, but curious, she asked, "Is this an important friend, Ursula?"

Surprised at the inference in her question, Ursula coughed and pet the dragon and cat who had curled up at her feet. Finally looking at Susan, she answered honestly, "Mergan is a very old and very dear friend who is indeed very special to me." Then, changing the subject, she said, "You have raised such an intelligent, kind young lady, Susan. You have so much to be proud of. Having a daughter turn from a child into a teenager has to be a challenge, for both of you."

When Susan sighed and nodded, Ursula continued, "Whitney's intelligence would tend to make her question things more than most. However, from what I've seen, you have an amazingly close relationship. That, above all else, will help you both get through this awkward period of time. I've noticed how easily you can talk with each other." She patted Susan's knee and said, "Whitney's been excited to see you from the moment she got out of bed this morning! As you are well aware, her excitement is quite contagious."

Just then her daughter came bounding through the door balancing their drinks, a box of chocolate chip cookies and treats for the little dragon and cat. Susan smiled at Ursula and whispered, "I know exactly what you mean. It's quite a treat, isn't it?"

They got caught up on Susan's exciting week. She admitted how surprised she was to be so comfortable speaking to a huge lecture hall full of people all looking up at her. In fact, she was proud to announce they'd asked her to return next year. Both Whitney and Ursula clapped at her success and Whitney said, "See mom, now everyone knows something I've known forever. You're amazing!"

Ursula stayed for lunch then picked up little Aiden and announced it was time for her to depart. Refusing their offer for a ride home, she waved and headed down the stairs to the beach with Aiden and her small suitcase saying, "I welcome the exercise. See you at Whitney's Thirteenth Birthday Party next Saturday!"

Standing there, arm in arm, Whitney and Susan waved to their friend and watched until she was a little speck in the sand then walked up to the deck. Sitting down in their favorite chairs, mother and daughter simply enjoyed each other's company as the sun moved closer to the horizon and late afternoon. Their conversation paused occasionally, and in the comfortable silence, they gazed out over the expansive view of the lake, one they never tired of. At the moment, both were feeling incredibly content and lucky they could share special moments like this.

However, a short while later, the weather turned from sunny and warm to cloudy and windy and the temperature dropped twenty degrees. Susan and Whitney decided to move indoors for an early dinner. It turned out to be a great decision, because the rain began while they were eating.

Moving to the fireplace after dinner, they enjoyed getting caught up on their week's adventures while working on their puzzle. It had been a long day, particularly for Susan with her early flight then long drive home. As they headed up the stairs, Susan suggested, "Tomorrow, let's plan for that very special thirteenth birthday coming up!" Thrilled at the opportunity to seeing her friends one more time, Whitney nodded her agreement.

Whitney and Ellie came downstairs to her mom humming a favorite tune while she cooked breakfast. Hearing her daughter enter the kitchen, she turned and smiled, opening her arms for a hug. Telling Whitney to sit down, she proceeded to put cat food into Ellie's bowl. Ellie was on it immediately, tail high and purring while she ate.

Bringing their eggs and bacon to the table, Susan sat down across from Whitney and shoved a long list and pen toward her daughter saying, "Let the party planning begin, my almost teenage daughter!" Smiling, Whitney was getting excited and told her mom that she'd already invited Edward, Ursula and Mergan, but asked her mom if she'd call Edward's grandparents.

Susan looked at her daughter wondering how and when Edward had been invited, but let it go for now. Her daughter had a glow about her that showed a remarkable transformation from the troubled girl she'd left just a week before. She would make sure to find out what had caused that, but simply wanted to bask in her happiness for the time being.

Their list was complete by the time breakfast ended. Whitney requested burgers and brats with coleslaw and baked beans for dinner, then one of her mom's famous peach pies for dessert, with ice cream of course! It would necessitate several stops in town for groceries, party favors and decorations. In addition, Susan wanted lots of colorful flowers in vases, and they didn't have many in their gardens at the moment, so that meant a trip to the florist too.

Whitney really wanted an outdoor party on the deck, especially with the "puppy" and Ms. Ellie running around, however they agreed they should clean the house as a back-up location.

Thinking that was wise, Susan admitted to herself the weather this summer was more unpredictable than any she'd ever experienced.

Not wanting to delay their shopping trip, Susan suggested they drive into town that morning to pick up the party favors. The rest could wait until later in the week. Excited, Whitney suggested they go to the jewelry store to see her friend Randolph, then maybe get some ice cream.

They left the party store with superhero themed party favors. Her mom had insisted on the theme, in honor of her amazing daughter. Whitney had pointed out other possibilities, arguing it was a bit too much and would likely be embarrassed the night of her party. Her mom was uncharacteristically insistent, however, so she finally gave up. Already dreading her Wonder Woman "W," head and arm bands, she silently vowed to take them all off as soon as possible!

The trip to the jewelry store was more fun, and Randolph was eager to show Whitney a stone he'd just purchased and told the folktale of its origin and powers. Always fascinated by Randolph's stories, Whitney was captivated. As they were preparing to leave, Susan asked him if he'd had any luck finding out who'd been in his store that day and he shook his head, a look of baffled bewilderment appearing on his pleasant face. Not wanting to upset him, Susan said casually, "Well I'm sure if an answer is to be found, you'll be the one to find it, Randolph," then waved good-bye. Leaving the store, Susan snapped her fingers and said, "Whitney I almost forgot something. You go on down to the ice cream shoppe and I'll meet you there in a few minutes, okay?" Nodding, she waved to her mom and walked through town slowly, feeling carefree and happy.

Susan rushed back into the jewelry store and brought out the aquamarine stone she'd purchased while at the conference in Colorado. Approaching Randolph who was still at the counter they'd just left, she put it in his outstretched hand.

"I'd like to put this little beauty on a simple 16" gold chain for Whitney and I'd like for it to hang right here," and pointed just below her collar bone. "It's so beautiful and delicate and I think it'll look nice sitting just above her necklace with the other three stones."

Agreeing it would be beautiful, Randolph said he could have it ready in just two days. Thanking him, Susan raced out the door thinking that would be perfect. She could pick it up when she returned to town for the groceries and flowers. Humming as she walked quickly to the ice cream shoppe, she couldn't wait to celebrate her lovely daughter in just six days.

# Chapter Twenty-Four

# THIRTEENTH BIRTHDAY PARTY

The house and back deck were both ready for their guests. Whitney and Susan had cleaned the entire house the day before, but it hadn't been necessary. Today was perfect for an outdoor party. The day moved toward late afternoon, as the sun dipped lower in the sky, however the temperature was still in the 70s and there was just a slight breeze. "How lucky are we to have such a rare and beautiful evening for your thirteenth birthday party!" Susan said happily.

They'd put out little lanterns with lights and colorful flowers in vases decorated the deck railing. The bright red umbrella was cranked wide open and spread shade over their wooden dining table and its red and white striped chairs with deep cushions. Susan had put a smaller table for gifts and cards by the door leading into the kitchen, with a fountain that had pink lemonade flowing from the top into a bowl full of ice cubes and cut lemon wedges.

There was another small table that held veggies, chips and Doritos and several types of dips, along with cups, paper plates and silverware. Surveying everything one last time, Susan was happy with the results. It all looked as inviting as she'd hoped. Hearing the sliding door to the deck open, she turned as her 'Super Daughter' walked out. Instantly stunned by her daughter's beauty, she said somewhat sadly, "There's my superhero daughter. Let me take a look at you." Pausing to watch her daughter twirl, she continued. "You look older, Whitney! Does turning thirteen do that to all daughters?"

Whitney was surprised to see a hint of sadness creep into her mom's intense scrutiny and gushing praises. Trying to lighten things up, she pointed to her Super Woman stuff, including the BIG 'W' on her T-Shirt, gold headband and arm band of 'power.' "Only those who are 'Super Daughters!'"

Although her eyes shone with unshed tears, Susan smiled brightly and grabbed two colorful flowers from one of the vases. Weaving them into their hair, she said softly, "I'm so proud of you, Whitney. You are my 'super daughter' each and every day and fill my life with such joy." Wiping at a stray tear, she smiled brightly. "Let's have some fun tonight!"

Just then, they heard "Yoo-Hoo!" from the bottom of the stairs and ran over to wave. There was Ursula with Aiden in her arms and a rather attractive man standing next to her. Ursula waved excitedly, then they both walked up the stairs quickly with little effort. As soon as they reached the deck, Susan noticed that neither were the slightest bit out of breath and thought, "I really need to find out what they do to maintain such energy and vitality!"

Ursula held out her arms for Whitney to run into, and little Aiden bounced up and down on Whitney's leg trying to get her attention. Laughing, Whitney picked up the little dragon and said a warm hello to Mergan.

Ignoring Whitney's sudden shyness, he pulled both her and the little dragon into his arms for a hug. Then Susan was pulled into Ursula's arms and introduced her friend, Mergan, who held out his hand saying, "It's a pleasure to finally meet you, Susan. You have such a wonderful daughter. I certainly enjoyed getting to know her while you were at the conference."

Susan thought his mannerisms and vocabulary were quite stiff and formal, however, she liked him immediately. "Maybe because he likes my daughter so much," she admitted to herself.

Noticing they had gifts, Susan led them to the gift table then headed to the lemonade fountain. Filling their cups with ice cold lemonade, they walked to the table and sunk into the soft chairs with a sigh of contentment. After taking long refreshing sips of the cool delicious drink, they smacked their lips and murmured, "AHH!" in unison. Then Ursula said, "You have the most beautiful decorations. Those cut flowers really make everything look festive!" Looking at Whitney, she continued, "Wonder Woman Whitney, eh? Now I'm quite certain that was Susan's idea. Am I right?" At both of their nods, she continued, "Susan, I think it's a perfect costume for Whitney. She is truly a wonder, in every way possible!"

Aiden and Ellie announced the arrival of Edward and his grandparents by racing each other down the stairs to the beach. While shielding their eyes from the setting sun, they all waved to the three walking toward the stairs.

It took Edward's grandparents far longer to walk up the stairs than either Ursula or Mergan, but with Edward's patient assistance, they eventually made it. However, as soon as they reached the deck, they stopped to catch their breath. Hugging Ursula, they were introduced to her friend, Mergan then walked to the gift table and added their presents to the growing pile. After pouring lemonade into cups from the fountain, Edward's grandparents joined Susan, Ursula and Mergan at the table.

Of course, Edward had to say something about her costume, but Whitney had expected no less from her friend. "Hey, Wonder Woman, did you create this perfect weather with your magic wand?" Ready with a comeback, Whitney replied, "Yep, but I don't use a wand. That's old-school! I used my handy-dandy gold band here and whipped it up just for us!"

Everyone laughed and Susan turned on the grill for the burgers and brats. Welcoming something to do, Edward once again volunteered to take over for Whitney's mom. Susan was grateful for the help, so she passed the spatula, and played hostess with ease and confidence. Watching her mom, Whitney hoped she'd feel so confident one day.

Wandering over with a glass of lemonade for Edward, Whitney laughed when a sudden burst of flames threatened to make charcoal out of their dinner. "Are you intentionally trying to burn our dinner?"

He'd momentarily taken his eyes off their dinner to watch Whitney. Somehow, she looked older tonight, and pretty cute as 'Super Woman.' Startled at the sudden burst of smoke and flames, he quickly pushing the meat away from those pesky flames, and sheepishly admitted he had to watch it more closely. Grateful to see the flames return to normal, Edward relaxed and took a drink of lemonade. Looking at his training partner, he admitted, "I've missed our training sessions." When she nodded her agreement, he continued, "You are more of a Wonder Woman than your mom knows. You didn't tell her anything about last week?"

Whitney shook her head, "I feel terrible leaving her out of my life like that, but no, I haven't said a word. Each time I was tempted, I'd remember Ursula and Mergan reminding us over and over that those we love will remain safer if we keep them out of this whole business. That always took away the temptation." Looking carefully at her friend, she added, "It makes perfect sense that we keep my mom and your grandparents in the dark, doesn't it?"

Edward nodded just as Susan walked up to see how the 'master chef' was doing. Inspecting his work, and thanking him profusely for a job well done, she announced, "Dinner is served!" That brought everyone up to fill plates and enjoy what Mergan called a 'marvelous meal.'

Disappearing for a few minutes, Whitney's mom emerged with Whitney's pie decked with thirteen sparkling candles and ice cream, singing "Happy Birthday." Everyone joined in, then Ursula clapped her hands then continued with, "Are you 1, are you 2..." prompting everyone to join in once again until Whitney laughed stopping them at thirteen.

After dessert, it was time to open presents. Whitney was thrilled at her pile of gifts. They were so beautifully wrapped and just beckoned for her to rip them open. Before she started, however, Edward slid near her and whispered, "Don't look inside mine until you're alone, okay?" She promised immediately but was now extremely curious and wondered to herself, "What on earth is he being so mysterious about?"

Starting with Edward's grandparents, she ripped open a large box to find three books on rocks. One of them was all about Lake Superior Agates. Grinning at them, she joked, "How did you know?"

Mergan's big, long package looked interesting so she opened that one next. He explained it was a walking stick that might help her uncover rocks along the beach without having to bend over all the time. Joking, he held his back with one hand, and bent over as if in pain and said, "That's something I'd appreciate myself!" While everyone was laughing and distracted, Mergan came up to hug her and whispered, "I'll tell you what its REAL talent is later."

Next came Ursula's gift, which she put on immediately because it matched her outfit. She'd given her a white ball cap for her beach walks with a note that said, "Good guys wear white hats, and they always win!" Grinning, she hugged her friend and said, "Thank You, Ursula! I'm so glad you're my friend. You have the best view of life and make me smile!"

Two gifts remained on the table, Edward's and her mom's. Reaching for biker boy's, she ripped off the wrapping paper revealing a large bag with a dragon stitched into the side. Edward announced, "I thought you could use a bag for all your beach finds!" Thinking it was just about perfect, Whitney grinned at the hidden meaning behind his gift but simply said, "I'll use it tomorrow. Thanks!"

Finally, she reached for the two boxes from her mom, one large and one small. Opening the large box first, she pulled out a T-shirt that said, "Rock On" with a caricature of a girl holding her arm in the air with a rock in her hand. Running to her mom, she hugged her and said, "Is this from Colorado?"

Susan smiled and said, "It is, along with the little one still sitting over there."

Racing over to open her last gift, Whitney gaped at the little stone necklace inside the box. As she pulled it out, her mom came over to help her put it on and offer her a small mirror. Gazing at her reflection, Whitney whispered, "Mom, it's so beautiful and it sits so perfectly above the other three. Is it an Aquamarine?"

Just as her mom nodded, Ursula clapped her hands with excitement and ran up to get a closer view. Holding it in her hand, she said, "It's a beautiful Aquamarine indeed, and another very special stone. Would everyone like to hear the folklore about Susan's well-chosen gift?"

She was glad when they all nodded, because she'd planned to tell them anyway. "Susan, this is a perfect stone for Whitney's collection. You've heard how special each one is. If you believe the ancient tales, this stone has very unique powers too. Aquamarine is Latin for 'Water of the Sea.' It's always been seen as a talisman for wanderers and explorers, thinking it brought them good luck. In very ancient times, it was even believed to counteract the forces of darkness." She stopped to look at Whitney and nodded her head imperceptibly then continued. "This beautiful stone looks like the waters of Lake Superior on a calm sunny day, doesn't it? It's even said this stone can enhance the intuitive abilities of the person wearing it." Winking at Whitney, Ursula finished by saying, "My dear, it looks like no one's thoughts or feelings will be safe around you any longer, not while you wear this lovely stone."

Whitney's mom added, "The Aquamarine is also Colorado's State Gemstone. I thought of you when I saw it displayed in almost every jewelry store and knew you had to have it, dear teenager of mine!"

. . .

Evening darkened into night while Whitney opened her presents. The lanterns along the deck railing looked so bright and beautiful, and a full moon had joined her party, shining brightly over the lake. Sighing at the amazing view, Edward's grandparents reluctantly said it was time to head home. Thanking Susan and Whitney for another wonderful evening with good friends, Edward's grandma looked at her grandson with a twinkle in her eyes and asked, "Edward, you said you wanted to stay a little longer, but did you remember your flashlight?" When Edward blushed and nodded, their smiles broadened as they headed toward the stairs.

Ursula jumped up to walk them down telling the others she'd be right back. As they walked, Ursula asked, "Have you given any more thought to that house in town? I understand the price has gone down. The owners are heading to Florida this week and hope to get it rented before they have to leave."

Edward's grandparents looked at each other and smiled saying, "You're a mind reader, Ursula. We intended to bring it up earlier but got so caught up in Whitney's party we totally forgot. Yes, we'd like to rent their home, but we're concerned about the trailer over the winter."

Touching both their arms Ursula reassured them. "You just let me take care of that little matter. I happen to know the forest service director personally and I'm sure we can reach an understanding that will be to your satisfaction. I'll tell him to contact you with the particulars." Waving farewell, she hurried back up the long flight of stairs.

Watching her scurry up so easily, Edward's grandma mumbled, "I must ask her what kind of vitamins she takes!"

Returning to the deck, Ursula noticed Susan and Mergan were deep in a conversation about animal husbandry, but Edward and Whitney had watched her return. The time to say good-bye was approaching all too fast and they dreaded it. Whitney's eyes were shining with unshed tears and when Edward caught her watching him, he looked down at his feet.

Walking over, she pulled them into one of her famous bear hugs and said, "We shall meet again, of that I'm certain. I only hope it's under happier circumstances. Just in case I haven't told you lately, I'm so proud of you both." Whitney's effort to control her emotions vanished and her unshed tears burst out of her eyes to fall freely down her cheeks.

Wiping the girl's tears, Ursula continued, "Someday everything will make perfect sense to all of us. For now, smile through those tears, young Whitney, and remember everything happens for a reason."

Holding Whitney close to her side, Ursula looked at Edward and reminded him, "You both know what you need to do. I truly don't think you'll be bothered by those nasty creatures for quite some time. Our enemies are too busy countering our well-planned attacks. If and when they begin anew, you're both well prepared for what happens next. Always try to imagine yourselves as I see you so very clearly, as capable extraordinary young people with so much to care about and live for. Take good care of each other for me, will you?"

Edward swiped at his eyes and looked away in embarrassment. Just then Mergan walked up and patted him on the back then turned to hug Whitney. Smiling one of his rare smiles, he said, "I'm sure my former student and dear friend has just about covered all the good-bye words of wisdom. Therefore, I'll just say it has been one fine week together and I can't wait to meet again!"

"Whitney, that hiking stick is actually a nifty little tool I designed just for you. Remember how you used your hands to push away the threat coming at you? That wizard's staff will give you a little more force if you have to do it again. I'd keep it near at all times if I were you." That caused Whitney to throw herself into his arms and hug him tightly mumbling, "I'll miss you too!"

Staring at this exchange, Edward blurted out, "Whitney, do you know how lucky you are? Ever since I saw Mergan's, I've wanted one!"

Mergan laughed and answered, "Maybe one day, Edward. Maybe one day."

All the dishes were done, so Susan returned to the deck to relax. However, when she saw the group of four huddled together looking quite sad, she walked over to them looking concerned. "Why so glum? We're only saying good night, right?"

Ursula turned to Susan and wiped her eyes with her Kleenex. She announced sadly, "Mergan and I just got word that we must leave the states tomorrow. Not much notice at all, but it's import- ant and we mustn't delay. Mergan has a relative that isn't well, and we need to fly to her at once. At this point, we don't know any of the details, so we don't know how long we'll be gone."

At Susan's shocked expression, Ursula spoke soothingly, "You and Whitney have a wonderful place and wonderful life here by the shores of Lake Superior. Edward's grandparents just told me they'd be renting a house in town through the winter, so you'll be able to see each other often." That brought a smile to Susan's face.

Continuing carefully, Ursula asked, "Because we must fly, I have a huge favor to ask of you. Would you mind taking care of

Aiden while we're gone? He won't be a bother, and I brought all of his current medical papers with me, hoping you would agree. I wish I could say how long we'll be gone, but I can't. However, we'll try to stay in touch as much as we can."

Stunned speechless, Susan stared at Ursula's hopeful expression, then at her smiling daughter and answered, "Absolutely! We'd love to care for your young puppy. He and Ms. Ellie get along famously and I'm sure Whitney will love having more company on her beach walks."

Hugging a relieved Ursula, Susan continued, "I hope Mergan's relative improves quickly because I have a daughter who will certainly miss you!"

Edward took that opportunity to say a quick good night to Whitney's mom, grabbed his flashlight and followed Whitney, Ursula and Mergan down the steps to the beach, with Aiden and Ellie running up and down the beach enthusiastically. Ursula bent down to pick up her little dragon and whispered a secret into his ear. He looked at her as if he understood then reached his front paws out toward Whitney. Sobbing all over again, she took him in her arms.

Edward wrapped his arm casually around her shoulders and together they watched Ursula and Mergan walk away. They were way down the beach, no doubt headed to the portal, when Edward stepped away to look at Whitney and Aiden. Bending over to pick up Ms. Ellie, he said, "Looks like it's the four of us now, Whitney. We'll get through this and see them again one way or another. Remember I've got your back and I know you have mine!"

Putting Ellie back on the ground, he turned on his flashlight then walked toward his grandparents' campground. Watching him walk home, she thought. "Biker boy, you don't look quite right without your bike!"

Once he'd disappeared into the darkness, with only the light from his flashlight bouncing off the dunes, she put Aiden on the ground, squared her shoulders and wiped her eyes. Following the two rambunctious creatures back up the stairs, she wondered what her future would hold.

Walking onto the deck to see her mom waiting there with concern on her face, she piled into her arms and cried for a long time, soaking her mom's pretty top.

Susan held her daughter, stroking her hair while she sobbed. Susan was so glad that, although now she was officially a teenager, Whitney still needed her and that felt mighty good!

Giving her mom a hug of thanks, Whitney was grateful she didn't ask any questions. One day she'd be able to tell her everything, but not yet.

A short while later, they were sitting in comfortable chairs surrounded by twinkling lanterns. Sipping one more glass of lemonade, they watched the full moon rise higher in the sky. Its bright reflection shimmered on the surface of the lake, like a path along the water. Staring at the amazing sight, Whitney pretended it was showing Ursula and Mergan their way home and thought, "That's a perfect ending to my thirteenth birthday."

Yawning, Whitney and Susan said good night and walked upstairs to bed. Whitney hugged her mom once again and thanked her for a wonderful birthday celebration, then took all her amazing gifts into her bedroom and shut the door.

Opening Edward's bag, she saw a small box laying in the bottom. She reached in and pulled it out and untied the little bow. When she opened it, there was a note and a keychain with a key on it. The note said, "Dear Whitney, this is the key to my grandparent's trailer, just in case!" Pulling the keychain out, her eyes teared up once again to see engraved on one side, "I'll always have your back," with the image of a little dragon on the other side.

She tumbled into bed surrounded by her "kids." Ms. Ellie was already purring, apparently all too happy to share Whitney's bed with little Aiden.

Deep in thought, Whitney gazed at the full moon through her window. It reminded her of the magnificent light show on the beach and all the events that had followed. It seemed like such a long time ago.

Whitney vowed softly, "I have your back too, Edward." Thinking of Ursula and Mergan, she hoped with all her heart her very good friends remained unharmed and that they'd all reunite soon. She missed her friends already and couldn't wait to see them again. Unfortunately, it could very well be the escalation of disturbing events on Yagdi that forced their reunion. Their alliance would be powerful if war indeed broke out.

Their alliance of four had begun. An alliance of friends, worthy of cherishing and protecting, and one she was confident would last a very long time. Closing her eyes, Whitney whispered, "Now that's what I call a powerful friendship!" and fell asleep.

# GLOSSARY

**Aiden** = Meaning: "little fire." Young dragon from Yagdi. Child of Torryn and Araa. Will be ruler one day.

**Alliance** = A relationship among people that have joined together for mutual benefit. Members of an alliance are called allies.

Aquamarine = From the Latin word meaning "water of the sea," it is Colorado's state gemstone and has a color between blue and green. It's been used as a talisman for wanderers and explorers, thinking it brought them good luck. In very ancient times, it was even believed to counteract the forces of darkness.

Araa = Mother of Aidan. Meaning "rare and beautiful."

**Bluff** = A small, rounded cliff that usually overlooks a body of water.

Chosen One = One chosen at birth due to their extraordinary capabilities. Their "gifts" exceed normal talents.

Dragons = The mighty protectors of Yagdi.

Eye Agate = A rare agate stone that displays one or more circular concentric marks, known as "eyes." Formed over a billion years ago, they are some of the oldest stones on Earth. Folklore says they have magic to share and are known to detect evil and will find a way to warn the person wearing them.

Ice-Cold Stones = A sign or warning that danger is imminent, most importantly the battles on Yagdi are not going well, putting the lives of the "chosen ones" and the dragon in peril.

Lake Superior = Largest of the Great Lakes of North America, and the world's largest freshwater lake by surface area. It is 350 miles long (east-west) and 160 miles wide (south-north) with 2,980 miles of shoreline. It is the coldest, deepest, and highest in elevation of any of the Great Lakes. The lake's average depth is 489 feet, and at 200 feet, its water remains a constant frigid 39 degrees. Between late spring and late fall, the shore can be shrouded in fog when the land surrounding Lake Superior heats up much warmer than the water. There have been 350 shipwrecks, with most occurring during fall storms called "northeasters."

Mage/Magician = A Learned person who practices magic.

**Magic** = The use of special power to make things happen that would usually be impossible.

Mergan = A Mage from Yagdi and Traveller's Teacher.

Merlinite = A stone named after the wizard Merlin. It's usually black and white and combines characteristics of two other stones, agate and opal. Folklore says wearing it will attract powerful magic and good luck in one's life. It can be calming and identify dark thoughts and strengthen intuition.

**Mist Creatures** = Evil, red-eyed creatures that travel within the mist.

Moonstone = A semitransparent or translucent, opalescent, pearly-blue gem. Folklore claims this stone is formed by moonlight and contains a powerful "good spirit" within it. It is believed to bring you good luck.

Ms. Ellie = Ferocious Black Panther on Yagdi; Black Bombay Cat on Earth who lives with Whitney and her mother. A Protector. The Bombay cat is a rare breed with a short jet-black fur coat that's sleek and panther-like. Loyal, attention-seeker, active and curious, round short nose, and head with golden eyes.

Nightmare = A frightening or unpleasant dream.

Pen Pals = People who regularly write to each other, particularly via postal mail. Usually strangers whose relationship is based primarily, or even solely, on their exchange of letters.

Peninsula = A piece of land almost surrounded by water or projecting out into a body of water ending in a point.

Polar Bear = A large white bear, Ursus maritimus, of the arctic regions. "Nanuk" in Inupiat is symbolic of a strong protector. Several Inuit legends depict polar bears as humans in disguise.

Portal = A door, gate or entrance. First recorded in 1300, from a Medieval Latin word "portalis," meaning "of a gate."

Premonition = A strong feeling that something is about to happen, especially something unpleasant.

Protégé = A person who is guided and supported by an older and more experienced or influential person.

**Purmot** = A defensive or offensive move by certain "chosen ones" to forcefully push outward with both of one's arms to harness the strength of the wind. This action removes, or pushes away, your enemy. It can also be used to force something to move toward your enemy.

Quartz = One of the most well-known minerals on earth. The crystalline form is hexagonal in shape, looking much like a prism. It's quite transparent and has many colorful shades. Ancient tales say the crystal quartz was formed long ago from the breath of the White Dragon and holds magic. It holds a very positive energy and is seen as a protector.

Rockhounding = A non-professional study and hobby of collecting rocks, minerals, and fossils from the natural environment.

Staff = A thin, lightweight rod that is held with one hand. Traditionally made of wood, it is used by magicians for magical purposes.

Tentacles = A slender, flexible limb or appendage in an animal used for grasping.

Thunderstorm = Form in a type of cloud known as a cumulonimbus, or dark rain cloud. They are most likely to occur in the spring and summer months and during the afternoon and evening hours. It's an electrical, or lightning, storm during which you hear thunder and see lightning. A severe thunderstorm can bring flash flooding, fires from lightning striking Earth, hail up to the size of softballs, and winds up to 120 miles per hour.

Torryn = Father of Aidan. Irish for "Chief." Mighty ruler and protector of Yagdi.

**Transform** = The act of making a thorough or dramatic change in form.

Traveller = A Protector and Giant Polar Bear in her world.

Triathlon = An endurance multisport race consisting of swimming, cycling and running.

**Upper Peninsula of Michigan** = Also known as Upper Michigan, or the U.P. First inhabited by Algonquian-speaking native American tribes, then explored by French colonists. It's bounded mostly by Lake Superior to the north. Current residents are called "Yoopers" from UP-ers. The Straits of Mackinac separate it from the Lower Peninsula of Michigan, and the Mackinac Bridge spans the five miles between the two land masses. Completed in 1957, it is one of the largest suspension bridges in the world.

Ursa Major Constellation = The Great Bear, the most prominent norther constellation containing the seven stars that form the Big Dipper.

Ursa Minor Constellation = The Little, or Lesser Bear, the northernmost constellation, containing the stars that form the Little Dipper, the outermost of which, at the end of the handle, is Polaris, the North Star.

Ursula = A female name from a Latin word meaning "bear."

Wafting = A defensive or offensive move by certain "chosen ones" to wave one's arm in an arc through the air with fingers spread while touching a Merlinite Stone with the other hand. This action creates a protective barrier, or dome.

Warrior = Someone brave who is engaged in an activity, cause, or conflict.

Wurfing = Form of travel between worlds. A portmanteau, meaning it combines the form and meaning of two or more words, or blends. In this case, the two combined words are "world" and "surfing."

Yagdi = Traveller's World, "The Land of Dragons": Yandi, a Chinese Tribal Leader, was born from a mighty dragon, and Huangdi, a legendary tribal leader. Considered the ancestors of the Chinese People.

# ACKNOWLEDGMENTS

A beautiful dream in May of 2020 was the inspiration for *The Polar Bear and The Dragon*. An incredible group of professionals, family, and friends took this journey with me, providing insights and encouragement. Author Chelsea Flagg expertly coached me from beginning to end, and significantly contributed to my growth as a new author. Jaye and Marty Trapp polished much of my manuscript with meticulous and effective editing. Neil Walker provided expert feedback. My dear friend Pat Walker, and sisters Anne and Carol, read each new chapter and encouraged me to continue. Kelbey's feedback as a teen with exceptional language arts skills helped me create interesting and realistic characters. Mark Pate's incredible illustrations breathed life into each character. And Mission Point Press patiently led me through the publishing process and artfully created a beautiful book. Finally, a very special thank you to my husband, Dave, for welcoming Whitney and her friends into our home as members of our family. His encouragement and great ideas kept me moving forward each and every day. I thank everyone from the bottom of my heart for helping my dream become a reality!

# ABOUT THE AUTHOR

Debbie Watson lives in Northern Michigan with her best friend and husband Dave and their two dogs, Parker and Buddy. As often as possible, they drive across the Mackinac Bridge, or "Mighty Mac," to camp and look for agates along the shores of Lake Superior. The rugged beauty and solitary spaces of that largest of all the Great Lakes is the inspiration for the setting of her book, *The Polar Bear and The Dragon*.

Always an avid reader, becoming an author has felt like a natural progression for Debbie. Her favorite authors cleverly draw her in and hold her captive from beginning to end. They thrill her with brilliant schemes and memorable characters who learn valuable life lessons. They charm her imagination. Debbie now hopes to create one of those memorable stories for her readers. One that lures them in, expands their imaginations, and maybe even nudges them to become writers one day. Cheers to great books!

Visit Debbie Watson online at debbiewatson.net.